THE
FATHERS OF ST. A.

THE
FATHERS OF ST. A.

Haydn Hasty, Ph.D.

To order additional copies of this book, contact:
Xlibris Corporation
1-888-795-4274
www.Xlibris.com
Orders@Xlibris.com
20111

CONTENTS

This book is dedicated to Franklin Martin,
Louis Hayden, Kenneth Speegle, Andrew Simmonds,
David Tate, Walter Chambers, Gordon Shumard,
William Stetson, Tom Brice, Kenneth Jones, Pattee Kirby,
Talbot Wilson, Fred Ladd, Donald Chapman,
Alan McDowell, the monks of the Order of the Holy Cross,
and the other men through the years who created the magic
of St. Andrew's Episcopal School for Boys.

PREFACE

Confrontation at Caen, France

I did not deserve this nightmare.

It began when I was fourteen years old, a couple of months after Nolan died. Once it began, it would not stop. I just wanted it to go away so I could forget. But I could not.

I had never been to France nor had I read about it. I knew no one who spoke French. Raised Southern, I held no intellectual aspirations. I was just a regular kid who wanted to play baseball for the rest of his life.

And as often is the paradox of life, things would turn out much differently than I could imagine. But I was fourteen years old, and I did not know any better. I learned to lie to myself first and then to others about my hurts, my fears, my wounds, and I hid from them, hoping they would go away and would not find me out. Hope was nothing less than an abstract theory.

In my dream, I am in the general vicinity of Caen, on the coast of Normandy, and I fight for the Résistance. I speak French, understand German, and dabble in Italian. I am around the age of twenty-three, unmarried, with no discernible family. I am part of a small band of other Résistance fighters whose lives are lived moment to moment and, at times, breath by breath.

There is no end to the killing and the horror. We hear of a future invasion but do not know if it will ever come. If there is anything of which I am certain, it is that today may be my last.

In my life, bodies are piled upon bodies, blood and entrails a part of the next step. So maimed, so very broken, so unconsciously violated are they. It is madness and I am a part of it. I, too, kill because it is expected and because I am angry at what the enemy has done to my country.

I meet my comrades in a small cottage that is bordered in the north by tall hedgerows, a slightly, sloping pasture to the west. It is an abandoned, war-torn skeleton of a small farming house. The family that lived and worked these fields has long since gone. In the hallway, under the planks, covered by a tattered, oval rug, rifles and grenades are retrieved and handed out. The plan is well laid out and the objective is clear.

We sprint out of the house across the pasture into a well-traveled forest where a mile later, we take cover behind a waist-high rock wall that borders the next open field. As we position ourselves behind the rocks, we soon freeze, suffocating all sound. We will initiate and complete this bloody massacre quickly.

Within moments, a German patrol of ten to twelve men is seen in the distance, moving mechanically and unknowingly to their deaths. My breath comes to a near halt as I check my weapon for readiness and wait. Upon the signal, I will do what must be done with hatred and malice. I will fulfill my role.

I lay the gun down beside me to wipe the perspiration from my brow and to clear my sight. I can hear their movement now and think only of my aim. There is no turning back and I am a good shot.

As an act of safety, I turn to my left to see my comrades around me. To my horrifying discovery, they are gone. I turn back to my right to face the same shocking truth. I am here alone. I look everywhere and there is no one. My weapon is nowhere to be found. I am not going to not survive this. I am going to die.

Terrified, I begin running back in the direction of the cottage, the patrol spotting me and taking chase. In a futile effort to survive, I seek refuge in a closet in the cottage. It is the act of a helpless child.

I stand frozen, my chest exploding, trying desperately to control my breathing when I hear the German patrol entering the cottage. I am dying of fear, terrorized by an enemy I am now powerless to confront.

I hear the footsteps of several men enter the room, the intentional and deadly movement of calculating men. One of them whispers, *"Da ist er."*

As I now begin to suffocate under the weight of my inevitable death, I hear the cocking sound of a German Luger pistol and know that it is leveled head-high, awaiting my decision as to the moment of my execution. One man, surrounded by others, anticipates my exit, calmly waiting, calmly focused on my death.

I awake terrified, sweating, sometimes crying. Always breathless, I am hardly aware of the illusion of the moment and the absence of the German soldiers. Sometimes, I wake up in my bed; sometimes, I do not know where I am. But as the moment expands into the next, I come to the understanding that I am still alive and have not been killed, yet. And with an infantile sense of safety, although I have survived this fight, I know I will face the German patrol another day.

I remind myself as I desperately try to fall asleep again that I did not ask for this. With no recourse, I am just another casualty of an endless war.

I do not want this in my life. I do not want to fight any longer. I just want to be left alone and play baseball for the rest of my life.

CHAPTER 1

The Leaving

In 1953, two years after Sam and I were born, Mother was divorced, burdened with our survival. Before I ever knew my father, he vanished. I retained no conscious recollection whatsoever of his physical or emotional features. Five years later, Mom married Nolan.

Prior to that catastrophic event, I have few memories of anything. Lincoln-logs, getting my mouth washed out with soap, getting in a fight on the first day of school in the first grade that resulted in a scar on my right elbow, and a rabid dog that chased Sammy and me up a rotten oak tree scarred by a bolt of lightening. This lack of memory has the texture of a heavy blanket, obscuring the good and the bad.

Nolan remained our stepfather for seven years until his death. We were told he died in an industrial accident. I believed that whatever it was, he got what he deserved and gave it no more thought. All I really knew was that he was no longer there to inflict his eternal punishment.

By the time a year had passed, Mother had lost her ability to discipline her two bucks, and we were becoming dangerously testy. I remember perfectly the day that our family crossed the threshold from which we would never withdraw. Mom and Sammy were arguing.

"What did I tell you? How many times do I have to tell you?" Mom screamed at him.

"What difference does it make to you, anyway? What the hell difference does it make? I'm sick of . . ." Sam never finished.

She swung all ninety-eight pounds of her narrow-hipped torso around as if delivering a crosscourt forearm and slapped him so hard across the face that the shadow of her hand was left plastered on his jaw. I could only make out three fingers and knew she slightly missed.

Sam was stiff, armored, and his eyes looked right through the top of her head as he slid a soothing, calm hand across his own printed skin.

"Must have been a fly in the room," he muttered, glancing around the kitchen slowly.

He was motionless. He stood defiant and focused.

At that instant, the three of us knew that she would never again be able to use the only weapon available to her to put us in our places. It was a moment of departure for all of us.

I quietly walked out of the house hoping not to attract her attention, leaving my twin brother to deal with the turmoil. He would be fine. This moment was insignificant and trivial to both of us. It would not even warrant a conversation. For both of us knew much worse.

As I passed the field that marked the edge of our property, I remembered an afternoon with Nolan from only a year before.

"Billy, get your glove. You're going to throw seven innings," he said.

I walked to my room reluctant but compliant, grabbed my glove and followed behind him to cross the gravel driveway into the straw field. I walked on past him and took my spot on the red-clay mound he had built for us a summer ago. Without speaking, I began to warm up. I was allowed ten pitches before they really counted.

"Outside, ball one."

"Outside, ball two."

I concentrated, not wanting to be out here after dark. Seven innings, nine strikes an inning, sixty-three strikes. Time passed slowly.

"OK," he said, "throw your curve ball."

I stepped back, rubbed the ball on the thigh of my jeans and stepped on the rectangular strip he had carved from a plastic container.

I squatted a little lower, my legs beginning to coil, tightening my two fingers along the seam as I suddenly felt my rage at him for all that he had perpetrated on me. As I began to glide toward my delivery, I threw a fastball as hard as I could at his head.

Rising slightly upward, the ball grazed the top of his mitt, struck the very top of his forehead and bounced across the road into the neighbor's yard.

"I said a curve ball, goddamnit!" and instantly, he was on me.

"Didn't you hear what I said!" as he struck me on the side of my head with an open hand, knocking the tears out in one swift blow.

"I thought you said fastball," I muttered, cringing, protecting my face.

As he walked back and took his place behind the plate, I balanced my fate with having delivered one blow in the name of justice. The raised seams of the old, weathered baseball left a red indentation on his forehead. That was enough for me. As far as I was concerned, a single blow to the head was getting off lightly.

Oddly, being on the mound was the only place I felt safe. One batter, seven guys behind me, and junk that Houdini couldn't throw made me feel invincible. I knew that I would win. Oh, did I love baseball. Sandy Koufax, Mickey Lolich, 'Big D' Don Drysdale, 'Say Hey' Willie Mays, and the likes were the Gods of my universe, the universe I governed with my imagination along with the Mickey Mantle cards stuck between the spokes on my bicycle tires.

That night, upon returning home for supper, I sensed that the house was quiet. Mother and Sammy had declared a truce.

I found a letter for Sammy and me on the kitchen table and my thoughts turned quickly away from my stepfather.

Dear Sammy and Billy,

I cannot say how pleased I was to receive reference blanks from St. Andrew's for you two. Pleased for several reasons. First, that you are interested, obviously, in laying a little better foundation for college and that you have enough sense to realize that such a school as St. Andrew's can get you on the right path. A lot of young men don't have enough sense to think of this until it's too late.

I am fully aware of the fact that your father's absence has probably had a maturing influence on both of you—which is as it should be. Once or twice, while I was up there, I started to pull you both off to the side for a "fatherly talk" —but I decided that you would get perhaps too much of this as time went along anyway—and that you were going to have to learn to stand on your own two feet, make your own decisions with your mother's help, and that the only way to do this, is just to get at it—laughing at your mistakes and going on. Thank God Nolan was there to step in your father's place and guide you.

St. Andrew's is a fine school. I used to work there every summer when I was in Sewanee, for at that time, we held many of our summer youth camps there. The school has a good academic standing and a good athletic reputation, so since you are both good in athletics, if you'll go up there and work, college scholarships will be available later.

I lost my father when I was a junior in high school and I know that it takes an about-face in attitudes and direction to cope with it. Having to leave home was the hardest part— particularly since I was madly in love with a girl at the time and thought that my whole world would collapse when I left. Needless to say, my world didn't collapse—it changed, but a new one took its place—and this was probably the best thing that ever happened to me because I started to grow up.

St. Andrew's has a lot to offer both of you. Things that you could never get anywhere else, and twenty years from now you'll both thank high heaven that you took advantage of it. Thank you for thinking enough of me to use my name. I hope my references help in some way in getting you admitted in the fall.

My best to both of you,
Father Charles Peters

"Did you see the letter from Father Peters?" I asked Mother when she returned home from work.

"Yes, he's a wonderful man. He cares a lot about both you boys."

"So, what exactly is happening now?" I asked.

"Uncle C is flying us to Monteagle day after tomorrow. You and Sammy will miss a day of school. You have your first interview tomorrow afternoon."

"Great," I moaned.

Uncle Charlie was a strong thread of fiber that was woven in and out of my life, always present at family gatherings, smiling, delighted to see me and possessing a quiet but dominant presence. He was a big man of coal-black hair and a small cowlick in the right corner of his scalp. Some people called him "C." He was a pilot for a local construction firm in Monroe. His father ran a shoe repair shop during the week and was a radio evangelist on Sundays on a local AM station. Although I had never flown before, I trusted Uncle C and looked at the trip as an adventure.

The adventure quickly turned into a disaster.

"Stop your crying right now!" Mother said, one hour into the flight.

"My ears are killing me! My head's going to explode!" I cried, holding my face in my hands. The pounding in my head was unbearable.

"Shut up, Billy!" Sammy yelled. "You're driving me crazy!"

"Up yours," I said.

Sammy kept punching me in the arm to silence my complaining, and the scuffling was driving Mother to the point of jumping out.

Uncle C stepped in. "If either one of you say another word, I promise you, you'll regret it! Now be quiet! Billy, we will be there shortly. Hold on."

We landed safely on an airstrip that was stuck out in the middle of nowhere on top of somewhere called Monteagle Mountain. You could see tire marks where there had been some drag racing and mud tracks at the other end where the speed had exceeded the length of the asphalt. A small, rectangular Coca-Cola sign that was unevenly hung and tilting to the right behind a cracked window read Monteagle Airport.

There was a St. Andrew's School van waiting for us as soon as we stepped off the plane, a smiling monk waving to us.

"Hello Billy! Hello Sammy! We are very excited about your visit! My name is Brother William. I am a monk in the Order of the Holy Cross."

"Hello," Sammy said.

"Hello, sir," I said, sticking my hand out.

As we settled in the van, Sammy asked, "Are you a teacher?"

"There is a group of us who live in the campus monastery," he said. "Most of us teach in one way or another. I teach physics and chemistry," he said, turning his attention to Mother. "Mrs. McNeal, if I didn't already say so, I'm very happy to meet you."

"Thank you," my mother said, smiling. "We are happy to be here. This is my brother-in-law, Charlie Medlin."

"What did he say he was?" I whispered to Sammy.

"I don't know. What difference does it make?" he said with nervous sarcasm.

Brother William quickly put us at ease with warm conversation and a sense of joy about our arrival in spite of our awkward and obvious nervousness.

"The ride to St. Andrew's," he said, "won't take but just a minute. We'll be at the entrance gates of the school in one curve, one railroad track, past the St. Andrew's post office that folks call Lackey's, and one-stop sign later."

I may as well have been in China. I had no idea where I was. But crossing the main road onto the campus, I was swallowed up in this carpet of pink and white dogwood petals that burst forth as in a resurrected dream of a time I had somehow known. When I spotted the first school blazer of maroon wool with the gold and white insignia, there were slivers of recognition flying across my mind. It seemed impossible to me that I somehow felt at home here.

Brother William introduced us to several people, pointed out a few offices, and led us directly to the office of the Headmaster, Father James Henry. While Mother was escorted into his office, Sammy and I were led off to meet a student who would show us around.

"Hi, what's your name?" the stranger asked, standing there in slacks, penny loafers, and a blue, short-sleeved shirt.

"My name's Billy McNeal, this is my twin brother Sammy."

"Nice to meet ya'," he said. "Y'all going to come to school here?"

"I don't know whether we're comin' here or goin' there. But I know we're going somewhere," Sammy said.

"It ain't bad here," he said.

"What's your name?" I asked.

"Steven Larue . . . some people call me Duck."

"Why?" I asked.

"Because I glide through everything. Just the way it is," he said, nonchalantly.

"Well, tell me something," Sammy asked, "if you were us, would you come to school here?"

"Yeah, I mean, there are things you deal with . . . being away from family and girls aren't so hot . . . but hey, it isn't so bad. I've been in worse places."

"What are the athletic teams like? Are they any good?" I inquired, as we walked in cadence along the black asphalt sidewalk leading away from the main campus.

"We usually get our ass kicked in football, we hold our own in basketball and wrestling, and baseball's not bad at all. All the pussies play soccer and tennis. Here, you've got to make the grades but it's better to be an athlete, because that way you got your guys behind you. I mean it's great to make good grades but if you don't play ball, then you're just another fucking dipwad. You've got to play ball. Either of y'all play ball?"

"Yeah," I answered, "both of us will probably play three sports a year."

"But not soccer or tennis," Sammy added.

"You'll do fine. No, really, you might like it here. It ain't that bad."

He took us through the dormitories and there wasn't a soul to be found. The rooms were immaculate and the bathrooms gave off the smell of pine-scented cleaner.

"This is my room," he said proudly as we stepped in.

His dorm room was decorated with a confederate flag, a mining hat that reeked of sulfur, two posters of Jimi Hendrix, and a Sewanee Military Academy cadet's hat hanging on the corner of the mirror with the words, "Gimps Blow."

"Sewanee Military Academy is our rival. Actually, SMA is a school for assholes, assholes that couldn't get into school anywhere else. I hate those bastards. We call 'em Gimps. When you walk by 'em in town, you spit on 'em. When you ride by 'em on the bus, you give 'em the finger. It's no big deal. They hate us, too," he explained almost instructionally.

"Sounds like fun," Sammy said.

"C'mon, I'll show you the gym," Steven said, slapping me on the back.

When we walked in, I was overwhelmed.

"God, this is beautiful," I said, trying not to show my excitement and awe. "This is the biggest gym I've ever seen."

"There's a bunch more downstairs," Steven said. "Everyone has their own locker and there's a gymnastics room and other stuff on the bottom floor."

We stood in front of the trophy cases and let our eyes ramble through the last thirty years.

"Boy," I said, "this is really nice. I would love to play in this gym."

As we continued our excursion by walking by the football and baseball fields, Duck pointed out the direction of Piney Point.

"It's really beautiful . . . overlooks the valley. You can see the Sewanee golf course. But you can also die. If you fall off, you ain't gonna get a second look. Seems like there's always some dipwad that does something stupid out there."

"Well, let's go out there. Is it far?" I asked.

"There ain't enough time," Duck explained. "C'mon . . . I'll show you Deep Woods."

We walked side-by-side past Hughston Hall where we soon came to the edge of the woods.

"You see that path? That'll take you out to Deep Woods. There's some evil shit goes on out there, so you have to be careful. There's still moonshiners and car theft gangs out there . . . least that's what Speedy says," he explained.

"Who's Speedy?" Sammy asked.

"Mr. Speedy Spangler is the discipline officer. He's a great guy but don't goof off or he'll go NNOKI on your ass," he explained. "We call him 'Speedy.'"

"What did you say?" I asked.

"I said he'll go NNOKI on your ass. Notify next of kin, idiot. It means he'll paddle you and you'll wish you were dead."

"I think I want to avoid that," Sammy said.

After an hour, Duck led us back to the administration office where my mother was standing with Father Henry.

"You see that priest, that guy with your mother? You see him?" he pointed out.

We nodded yes.

"Yeah, we met him when we got here. He's the headmaster, isn't he?" I asked.

"Yep, that's the Czar. Father Henry. The man rules the roost. We call him B-Czar because when he gets mad, that pointed nose and mouth turn real red and makes him look just like a buzzard. He's really OK. But when he's pissed, he's no priest, so stay out of his way. I like him, though," Duck said.

"He looks real smart," I said.

"Hell, yes, he's smart. He's got a master's degree. Went to the Citadel and Harvard. He teaches the advanced English class here. He knows every damn thing there is to know about English literature. I know. I'm in his class. And he don't take no shit, either. He kicked this one kid out the first week of class 'cause the dipwad showed up without his homework," Duck explained.

"Are all the teachers like that?" I asked.

"Let's put it this way . . . you'll get used to it. It ain't no big deal. You've got to learn to glide."

We rambled along the concrete sidewalk to the first step just below their gaze. An hour had passed unnoticed.

"Mr. Larue, thank you taking the boys on the tour. Did you show them the gym?" said Father Henry.

"You're welcome, Father, it was a good break for me. I showed 'em."

"Showed *them*, Mr. Larue, *them*," he smiled.

"Yes, sir, I showed them all of it, even how to get to Piney Point and Deep Woods, too," Duck said.

"Well, fine. Boys, come in my office and Mr. Larue, you may head back to class. Thank you once again, Steven."

"Oh, you're welcome, Father," he replied, as he started to turn away.

As Father Henry and my mother moved inside, I turned and whispered to Duck, "Maybe we're going to come here next year . . . maybe we're not."

"I have a feeling you're going to," Duck said.

"Me, too," I smiled.

"What's your name again?" Duck asked.

"Billy. It's Billy McNeal."

"I'll try to remember that. See ya', man."

"You're Steven?" I asked.

"Duck," he said without turning around.

I didn't think for a second that he would remember me.

"Thanks. See ya'," I said.

He lifted his hand in the air, waved, and was gone around the corner.

Nervously, we stepped back inside the main door of the administration building on glowing slabs of polished slate, our squeaky, hard-soled shoes clicking rhythmically along. Instead of leading us to his office, he led us to the Hawkins Room, the Honor Board room where the names of each year's brightest and most athletic students were printed on leather paneling.

Without really understanding the magnitude of this room, I

was full of reverence at this sight. Father Henry was boastful like one of their fathers. He spoke emotionally like one of their mothers. And he was serious as though he was the appointed guardian of this sacred order.

As I stood there, I felt so small in front of those names and wondered what it could possibly be like to be immortalized like that, to have my name written in golden ink along with the names of these great ones. Walking almost backwards out of the room, his eyes remained pinned to the board.

He finished his elaboration by saying, "We are proud of all of our boys."

I could tell he meant it.

His office mirrored success and commitment. The whole room glowed with honor and masculine decor. Sam and I sat down and became still, our eyes focused on the man.

"Boys, we would be happy to have you join us next year."

"Sir, does this mean that we are coming to this school next year?" I asked.

"Yes, Billy. In fact, if you choose to play football, you will be reporting the 27th of August. But above all, I want you to know that you will succeed here and do a fine job. I want you to know that I expect the best from both of you and you can expect the best from St. Andrew's."

There was little else to say. Mother wore a Kodak smile. She had succeeded.

On the way out, I realized that the exit gave no clues to its direction back to North Carolina. What I did know, as soon as we passed through those front gates, was that I would return to St. Andrew's in August of the upcoming summer. At the precise moment that I was heading home, I knew somewhere inside I was leaving it forever.

———————————

"In the years that I have lived, which, according to court house records, are thirty-nine, but which, at times, I am convinced dire errors were made in, give or take twenty years, depending on what kind of day it has been, there have been numerous things I have said both to myself and aloud to others that I would never do. These never-do things range in scope from eating cold turnip greens to getting a divorce. Well, the cold-turnip-green-never was taken care of when I found myself with two boys in diapers. And if you think I don't mean 'found myself,' let me assure you that I do. When you have a forty-eight-hour day and only twenty-four hours in which to do the work, you'll eat anything . . . hot or cold.

"One day I was a bride; eleven months later, I was the mother of two sons, twins, and the wife of a man who mysteriously turned into a three-year-old. And somehow, there wasn't much time in between the wedding and the lapse of eleven months for finding myself. The few times I did, it was under the daily wash of twenty-four diapers. In fact, it was in divorce court when the twins were two, when I was sitting on the witness stand stating my name, age and names of my dependent children that I 'found' myself' the mother of two.

"Well, to get back to the nevers. As the twins grew older and reached high-school age, I observed some of their friends being sent away to school. I often made the remark to my friends that, 'One thing I would never do would be to send any of my boys away to school.'

"By January of the following year, our family situation had not improved much, but certain things were becoming apparent in our home. The boys needed to be around a man. Everyone had stood up splendidly under the strain of not having a father, but now the unraveling was beginning.

"I don't know now if it was the effect of three beers and the boys being in bed asleep by nine thirty and having a few moments to think, or if it was just the hand of Divine Providence, but, at any rate, I decided I had to act.

"By April, their choice was narrowed to one school. In other words, their grades were not good enough to get into any other. Sam was a mite disappointed to learn this fact; Billy could have cared less. He had decided where he wanted to go on the basis of the new gymnasium that he had seen at the school, and the grades were of no interest to him, anyway.

"The time that led up to their actually leaving for school that fall was not completely uneventful, and no minor item on the list of events was the damage done to a savings account in the process of collecting the items the school requires each boy to have, as well as those that a mother is firmly convinced her sons are unable to exist without.

"The other outstanding event was Billy's last-minute love affair, which practically threw a monkey-wrench in the whole deal because he was so enamored of the young lady that he was convinced that he could not do without her for a day, an hour, or even a minute. And it was too late to pack her because the trunks had been shipped two weeks early. Before I knew it, my boys were gone."

Em McNeal, Fall, 1967

CHAPTER 2

New Boys and Early Football

The summer of 1967 was a frantic ordeal.

Mother took great pains to buy new wardrobes for both of us, sewing every stitch of clothing, every sock, every handkerchief, and every washcloth with a label that bore our names in light blue thread. She purchased two huge, black trunks that were big enough to hold all of our belongings and us, if necessary. Printed in silver paint on the side were our names and addresses at St. Andrew's School.

Mother received a form letter from Father Henry on June 24 of that summer, which discussed various aspects of school life such as the mandatory haircut every two weeks, $2.00 a week spending money, dismissal violations for smoking and drinking, dress codes, and the need for a school blazer. Our late August exodus was the complete focus of our summer.

"This is the first of the summer messages to you as parents of one of our new boys. May I say first that we are looking forward with much pleasure to our association with you and your boy. You will find that a close family relationship binds all members of the St. Andrew's family together, boys, faculty, and parents. We are all deeply concerned with the education and welfare of your boy, and you will come to see this concern and to know that we have a warmth and genuine love in our hearts and souls for him. You may find also, especially at first, that the school is somewhat strict and demanding in its academic and other requirements. Please realize that we are trying to give you and your boy the very best, and the best is never easy to obtain."

His last letter came one week before departure and was dated August 20, 1967.

"To the Parents of New Boys
"Dear Parents,

"Well, the time is rapidly approaching for the beginning of another academic year. I suppose by this time you and your boy are looking forward with somewhat mixed emotions to your first experience at St. Andrew's School. There is probably some excitement and confusion as you begin to make your final preparations. There may be a growing feeling of nostalgia and perhaps some uncertainty as you think about your boy going away and leaving the family home.

"I want to assure you that we will be doing our very best to take good care of your boy and to provide him with the very best of everything possible in a preparatory school education. The experience of hundreds of St. Andrew's boys over many generations have shown without any question of doubt that these years spent at St. Andrew's are among the most valuable in a boy's life.

"Hundreds of St. Andrew's boys look back on their school years with a feeling of deep involvement, with cherished memories, and with a fond longing to return. We hope and trust and feel sure that you will never regret your decision for your boy to attend St. Andrew's.

"We are certainly looking forward with pleasure to having your boy with us, and I hope that I will have an opportunity to see you and meet you in the very near future."

I was lying on my back on my bed that evening when Mother came in.

"Honey, what are you doing?" she asked.

"Nothing . . . nothing," I said in an attempt to avoid a probing conversation.

"Are you nervous about leaving?" she inquired more intentionally.

"No, not really. I'm OK with going. I'll miss the dogs and some of my friends. I'll miss home, I'm sure," I said.

"What do you think you'll miss the most?" she asked.

"I don't know . . . probably my friends . . . not like I have that many. I mean, Sammy's the one that's popular . . . not that I care . . . I think most of his friends are idiots."

"You and your brother have two different ways of looking at things," she explained. "I have no doubt that you will do well. You owe it to me and to yourself. But most of all, you owe it to Nolan. He loved the two of you so much."

"I'm sure," I said, "that I will do well. I worry a little about the academic stuff but it's OK. I'll be fine."

"Pick your clothes off of the floor and c'mon to the table. Supper will be ready in five minutes."

I turned on my side, away from my brother's bed, and pondered my future. The only constant was change itself.

Uncle C, Aunt Tootie, Momma, and Aunt Evelyn accompanied Sammy and me to the airport on the late afternoon of Sunday, August 26, 1967. Teardrops the weight of mercury formed in my eyes as I turned my back to them to leave and board the plane.

Close to my sixteenth birthday, I could not know my mother's feelings, whether it was by choice or force that she was letting us go. It simply did not matter. Nor was she capable of knowing mine. When the door to the Eastern Airlines plane was closed and everyone was out of sight, I sank in my seat and held back my tears.

"If I end up getting pushed around by somebody, are you gonna help out or are you gonna sit there with your finger up your ass the way you . . ."

"Shut up," I said to Sammy, looking out the window, choking down my tears.

"I mean it, Billy. If I get in some trouble, you better be there. You chicken out and I'll kick your ass," he said.

"Don't worry about it. Ain't nothing gonna happen. Just don't start running your mouth you way you do at home," I warned.

"Let me tell you something. You better worry about keeping your head glued to the rest of your body tomorrow morning. I got a feeling this football thing is going be rough," he said.

Sammy had played football for several years and he was fearless and stoic in the face of adversity. His was a learned behavior linked to his extraordinary ability to survive. I thought to myself, "I'll just imitate him."

The engine purred to a consistent pattern of louder to softer, and I recalled the first trip to St. Andrew's and the pain in my ears. Racing in my mind were the memories of North Carolina and home.

It suddenly occurred to me that I was taking it all with me. The memories were embedded in me like millions of tiny, shiny pebbles contained within the banks of a mountain stream. If I was naive enough to think that I would be able to forget what happened, then that thought would quickly enough be rendered powerless by the omnipotence of memory itself, of memory's ambition to remind and haunt. Only temporarily was I able to lock it away.

By the time we got to the Chattanooga airport, dusk had quietly settled. Brother Wade, another monk who lived at St. Michael's monastery, met us. He was as exuberant and outwardly demonstrative of his joy in having us at the school, just as Brother James had been.

Brother Wade was dressed as I imagined a monk to be with brown-corded belt and sandals. I wore a brand spanking-new pair of polyester blue trousers with a white shirt that was half-covered up by an atrocious, plaid tie that was about as wide as half of my chest, a Coke stain on the left side pocket from a spill on the airplane, and a pair of ugly, black, hard-soled shoes I polished for fifteen minutes the night before.

Sammy was dressed to the hilt as usual, with a red Banlon shirt buttoned all the way to the collar, gray cuffed trousers that had been home-starched, matching red cloth belt, and tasseled, brown loafers. His hair was perfectly combed and parted. Brother Wade was ahead of us, leading us to the baggage claim.

Sammy grumbled out of the corner of his mouth. "Jesus, Billy, I hope nobody sees us," Sammy said, cupping his mouth.

"He seems OK. I'd rather wear what he's got on than this shit I'm wearing."

"I'm not talking about him. I'm talking about you. What an idiot."

"Up yours, Sammy. Nobody cares what you're wearing. You just think they do. You think you're your clothes." We were at it again.

"Look at me and then look at you. What do you see?" Sammy sneered.

"I see a genius walking beside a moron."

"That's right, so shut up, moron," Sammy said, jabbing his index finger in my ribs.

"Boys, come this way and we'll get your baggage."

If Brother Wade heard us, he did not let on.

With some help from the skycap, we loaded everything in back of the school van. I gave the skycap one dollar as Mother instructed me to do and Sammy did the same. In a flash, we were rolling down the interstate toward our new home.

I asked Brother Wade a thousand questions and soon, Sammy was joining in.

"McCallie and Baylor schools are here in Chattanooga. They are Tennessee's athletic powerhouses against whom we have little chance."

"Do we play them in football? Sammy asked.

"If we did, I'm afraid everyone would be dead. There would be no one left.

They are much too big for us to compete against in football. McCallie is to Baylor what Sewanee Military Academy is to St. Andrew's. Bitter, bitter enemies. But we do play them in basketball, soccer, tennis, wrestling, cross-country and baseball."

Sammy and I looked smugly at one another when he said the last word.

"The downtown bus station is right up that hill and to the left. You can see Lookout Mountain in the distance in front of us," he said. "There will probably be times that you will need to hitchhike into Chattanooga and it's important to know how to get here."

And as the noisy van wound its way through the outskirts of the Chattanooga lights, dusk overtook the vehicle, and the city disappeared behind us. I was asleep in no time.

I awoke when my ears started popping and the chassis of the van was melting into the curves of Monteagle Mountain. I felt nauseated, leaning left, then right, forcing a yawn to regain equilibrium, cracking my jaws repeatedly.

Moments later, the bright, neon lights of the Holiday Inn sign stood out in the hazy, evening fog as the tires whined up the incline of the off-ramp. Ten minutes later, we were at the school.

No sooner had we gone through the entrance gates than I remembered that I had no idea how I really got here. My thoughts were cloudy with emotional fatigue and fear of the upcoming day. I had paid no attention to the roads and realized an escape plan was out of the question.

Sammy and I unloaded our suitcases at the quadrangle and were shown to our rooms in St. Patrick's dormitory. As we inched our way up the stairs, we could hear the voices of other boys who had arrived for early football. When I stepped through the door of my room, I saw that my roommate was already unpacked and settled in the top bunk, taking the desk and cabinet space on the right side of the room. His name was Mitch Abernathy from Greenville, South Carolina.

Sammy's roommate met him at the door.

"Hey, man, how are you doing? I'm Randall Watkins, Columbus, Ohio."

It was obvious from just looking at him that Watkins could have cared less about having left home. He was glad to be here.

"Doing real good. I'm Sammy McNeal, from Monroe, North Carolina."

"Who? What did you say?" Watkins asked.

"Sammy," he said calmly.

"So you're here for football, huh?"

"Yeah, that's my twin brother, Billy, over there."

I crossed the hall to shake hands.

"Jesus, you don't look at all like each other."

"I know," I said, "I've always been better looking."

"Up yours again," Sammy said.

"Have you been to school here before?" I asked.

"Nope, new boy. First year," he said. "My older brother graduated from here in '63 so I guess my parents figured that I ought to come here, too. Are you two new?" he asked, as if it didn't show.

"Yep. Real damn new," Sammy said. "Have you met any of the other guys?"

"Yeah, I met a lot of them. They seem pretty nice except one guy. He acts like a real badass. His name's Lizard or something. They say he's a prefect," Watkins explained.

About that time another boy came into view from the room next door to Sammy's, rambled into the space that the three of us were sharing, and blurted, "Don't worry about Lizard Baldwin. Stay out of his way and he'll stay out of yours," the old boy said. "I'm Nelson Goodyear, it's my third year here. I'm an old boy. How's everybody doing?"

So, we started over again with the introductions and the superficialities of who each one of us were, jockeying unconsciously and nervously for territorial footholds. Before long, the entire floor, consisting of only about the eight of us, had gathered in Sammy's room to shoot the breeze and prepare for the next day.

Mitch had joined us by then as each one in the group would leave momentarily to further unpack, to put on the fresh sheets that were stacked on top at the foot of the mattress, only to return to the group to join in the lying about girlfriends and summer triumphs.

At nine forty-five, a voice echoed throughout the hallway.

"Gentlemen, you have five minutes to get those lights off and keep them off. I'll be waking you at six fifteen in the morning for breakfast. Don't eat too much but get plenty to drink. Practice will begin with a meeting at seven thirty sharp in the gymnastics room. Now, let's get to sleep. You'll be glad you had your rest tomorrow."

As we exited Sammy's room and headed for our own, I saw a barrel-chested, leather-skinned man standing there at the end of the hall, smiling, a Pall Mall cigarette cupped in his left hand. He moved in our direction, sticking his head in each room on the right and left sides. He spoke to each new boy, introduced himself, and welcomed each one.

When he came up to me, I was struck with the thickness of his rawhide skin and his crooked smile. His pants' legs were sitting a good three inches out on top of his shoes.

"Son, I'm Mr. Spangler. Who are you?"

"I'm Billy McNeal and that's my twin brother, Sammy," I said nervously, pointing in Sammy's direction.

"Glad to meet you, boys. Which one of you's the ugliest?"

"He is," both of us said, signaling the other.

"That's what I thought," he said laughing. "Well, get plenty of sleep tonight. Billy, you haven't played before, right?"

"Yes, sir, that's right."

"Don't let it bother you, son. There's boys you'll see tomorrow that's been playing for three years and they don't do squat. You'll do fine."

"Thanks, Mr. Spangler. I hope I do."

Nelson yelled out, "Don't call him Mr. Spangler. Call him Speedy!"

I looked at Mr. Spangler for confirmation and thought for a brief second that Nelson was asking for trouble.

"That's fine, Billy. All the boys call me Speedy. It's all right."

"Sir, why do they call you Speedy?'" I asked.

"I hope you don't have to find out, Mr. McNeal," he said smiling. He patted me on the back and moved to the other end of the hall.

"Let's get our rest, gentlemen," he said. "Get your lights out."

The sound of Speedy's footsteps faded down the staircase, and the first night was upon us. My roommate leaned his head over the bunk and looked down at me.

"Seems a little weird," Mitch whispered.

"I know. Seems OK so far. I don't know how tomorrow's going to go. I've never played before," I said.

"Oh, you'll be fine. I saw a lot of the older boys earlier this afternoon and they look like shit. You'll be fine."

There was a pause and Mitch began again.

"So, why did they send you away?"

"Oh, I don't know. Neither of us was doing very well in school. Well, to be honest, I was the one that wasn't doing very well in school. Last year was the first year they integrated the schools and I reckon Mother was partly afraid that that I wouldn't get an education. Mom got to where she couldn't deal with us anyway. She said this was the best idea she could come up with."

"If you don't like it here, can you go home?" he asked.

"I have no idea," I said. "Why did your parents send you here?"

"Because," he explained, "they said I need structure," he said, as he rolled his eyes to the top of his head and hurled his extended middle finger into space, supposedly reaching all the way to Greenville, South Carolina.

I tried to cover my laughter by coughing.

"Do you have a girlfriend?" he asked, changing the subject.

"Sure," I said. "Do you?"

"Man, I always have a girlfriend but I don't think the prospects here are real inviting, if you know what I mean. My parents might come up to visit in a couple of weeks and bring my girlfriend."

"That'd be nice," I said. "I might ask my mother to do the same thing."

He crawled down the bed frame and sat on the end of the bed.

"Have you talked to your dad?"

"My dad?" I asked.

"Yeah, dipwad, your dad," he said.

"Sorry. I just didn't get it. See, I don't have a father," I said. "Do you?"

"How come you don't have a dad?" he asked.

"I don't know. I was never really told. My parents got divorced when Sam and I were two. I had a stepfather for a while, and he died when I was fourteen."

"Did you like your stepfather?" Mitch asked.

"No, I didn't," I said.

"Was he an asshole?"

"All of the time," I said.

"Well, who knows, maybe you'll meet your dad one day. Maybe he'll try and find you."

"I guess. I don't know," I said. "I never knew him so it doesn't make that much difference to me. Do you have a dad?" I asked again.

"Oh yeah, I got a dad. He's a real bastard sometimes but at other times, he's real good to me. He wanted me to call him tonight but I haven't had a chance."

Suddenly, he scrambled to his feet and Mitch Abernathy's first unrehearsed, one-act play began. Behind him, the curtains swayed, the evening moonlight darting in and out of the room.

"Letter for Billy McNeal! I have a letter for Billy McNeal from his dad!" he said, his arm outstretched, pretending to hold a letter. "What? You mean I have to go through the javelin field to get the letter to him?" he asked an invisible person.

"Oh God! Oh God!" he yelled. "S-s-s-s-u-u-u-p-p-p-p. A-a-a-a-h-h-h G-a-w-d," he moaned slowly, dying right in front of me, sucking the air in. His whole body went stiff. He made a gasping sigh and remained motionless, his arm still outstretched, his torso frozen.

"What are you doing?" I asked.

"That's my imitation of a mailman being hit by a javelin from behind," he explained. He still had not moved.

I laughed again and adjusted my posture.

"That's funny," I said. "You're weird, but funny."

"Got to laugh, I mean, this is our first night and tomorrow we're going to get NNOKIed. Better laugh now while we can." His seriousness returned.

"How did you learn that word?" I asked.

"Some kid called Duck. He said it means 'notify next of kin, idiot.'"

"I think you're right. I think we are going to get NNOKIed," I said, my seriousness returning as well.

We wrestled with idle conversation and called it a night an hour later. I lay awake, wondering what my mother was doing, how Sammy was handling this night across the hall, and whether or not the dogs had been fed.

Sadness filled my throat as I choked back what seemed to be an endless well of tears and I buried my face in the pillow to somehow draw enough strength to weather this single night of perceived sudden, savage isolation in a place whose location I could barely identify. My chest was empty of anything resembling courage, my legs drained of the energy to stand, and I was frightened.

I lay frozen until I trailed off to sleep and began again my unwanted trip to the coast of France. I awoke from the nightmare, startled and afraid. The bed sheets were soaked. Did I urinate in my bed or was I just sweating?

I slipped over the side of my bed and brailed my way to the bathroom at the end of the hall which was lit with a full moon reflecting its face across the row of mirrors, a lunar circle anchored low to the horizon through the tops of the pines.

The urine was a deep gold and the rank and putrid smell filled my nostrils. I leaned against the wall as I flushed the toilet and felt the cold tile against the balls of my feet. Staggering out, my eyes partially closed and staying close to the left wall, I inched my way down the hall and into my bed again. I sought out a drier spot on the mattress, and soon fell back asleep.

CHAPTER 3

In the Trenches

"Up and at 'em, boys. We got work to do! Let's go!"

The morning exploded with loud voices that blared and ricocheted off the dormitory walls.

It was Speedy again. I could barely make out whether it was light or dark. It took only seconds to get dressed and a group of us headed to the cafeteria. As we stumbled in groggily and nervously, we noticed a checklist on the table. A short line had formed with boys crossing out their names, yawning, some struggling to find the spelling of their names.

When I found mine, I turned around to Sammy and asked, "Are you McNeal I or II?"

"Don't matter. Just mark one of 'em off. I'll mark the one you don't."

No sooner had I reached for a serving tray and silverware than a dark-haired boy snuggled in behind me, put his arm on my shoulder, and said, "Well, son, what are you going to eat today?"

He was speaking with a fake hillbilly accent, and I smelled trouble. I tried to ignore him, but he pressed for an answer.

"I said, what are you going to eat?"

"None of your business." I turned my back to him.

"Oh, what have we got here?" he said. "Does my talking bother you?"

"I don't know. Does it bother you?" I said, recovering as quickly as I could.

"Just trying to help you out, a-hole," he said, turning away.

I chose silence as the best defense and moved as quickly as I could through the cold line. When I came to the hot food, I was greeted warmly.

"Well, good morning, son, you must be new!" the silver-haired lady said.

I was getting tired of being new here.

"I'm Granny and I'm ah gonna make sure you get enough to eat here sos' that you ain't gonna be ah runnin' 'round hungry. This is Mrs. Smith and Mrs. Foster," she pointed out. "What's your name?"

"My name is Billy McNeal. This is my first year here."

"Well, that's Jim Dandy, Mr. McNeal! Do you want some eggs and bacon? They're mighty good this morning!" she said pleasantly, obviously comfortable with her position in this herd.

"Yes, ma'am, please," I said.

"And good manners to boot! Don't let Coach Stevenson run y'all too hard, now. You can come back and get as much as you want. There you go," she said, handing me my first breakfast, the warmth of the plastic tray baking my fingertips.

"Thank you, ma'am."

"Billy, call me Granny," she said lovingly, knowing I was a zebra cub in this den of lions.

"Thank you, Granny," I said smiling.

As I stepped into the dining hall, my attention was diverted upwards from the aroma of my hot breakfast to the sight of the class banners that flew above on every side. I barely remembered seeing them from my first tour of the school.

It would be inaccurate to refer to them as banners. Rather, they were medieval tapestries, embroidered cloth of such rich design that you felt like you were dining in a royal court. There were fifty or more of them, mostly the same size, separated in equal distance, hung a couple of feet from the ceiling which itself spanned thirty feet upwards.

Sitting at the table, I traced the class flags of the boys who had passed through St. Andrew's, sewn memoirs hung on golden rods, some tattered and frayed at the edges. *Veritas Fortitudo Perserverentia. Peus et Veritas.*

"What are you looking at those stupid fucking flags for?" Mitch asked, "They're just up there for decoration. Shit, I could make one myself."

I laughed. "Yeah, you're probably right. But, look at that one. It looks like it is fifty years old. Man, that thing is old."

"Old? Not as old as them old geezers who come back for class reunions. Hell, I bet most of them guys are dead and six feet under by now."

"Probably," I said, biting into my hot bacon.

Just then, the same boy who spoke to me in the breakfast line sat across from me and I did not dare utter a single word even though he continued to stare and grin at me. I did the best I could to ignore him.

The St. Patrick's bunch rolled out of the cafeteria together, staggering back to the rooms to make our beds, straighten up, and gather a few final minutes of rest before the first session began. Fear crept steadily back into my legs and my stomach.

It was seven fifteen. Time to die.

Huddled together with Nelson Goodyear leading the way, we tramped across the quad to our first practice. Halfway down the rock-bordered path to the gym, Nelson tripped and tumbled forward, sprawling out face-first into the ground.

Our group erupted into laughter.

"God, Goodyear, what did you do, have a flat tire? Man, you were NNOKIed!" Mitch was amused.

"Fuck you, Abernathy. We'll see who's got the balance in about an hour."

"Just kidding, Flat Tire!" he said, bellowing like a cow.

"You're real fucking smart, aren't you Abe Lincoln?" Flat Tire roared back.

Thus, our new names were born. Rising upwards from deepening friendships, nuances, codes and innuendoes, known and spoken only by the tribe members. Flat Tire and the President would become loyal friends.

We were all amused and by the time we arrived at the gym steps, our laughter was abundant. On the gym steps was the same boy who had stood behind me in the cafeteria line.

"Where are you going to sit?" I asked Hollinbeck, another of our St. Patrick's crew.

"As far in the fucking back as I can . . . that's where," he said.

Like a school of fish, we darted together to the back, seeking anonymity.

Parked in the back seats of the gymnastics room, we waited nervously as the coaches pushed their way noisily through the squeaky, metallic door.

I spotted Duck a couple of guys down on my right.

"Hey, man, how are you doing?" I asked.

"Hey, Billy! I remember you. I knew you'd be here. I just got in late last night. I live over in . . ."

The door swung open and silence enveloped the room.

The head coach was Edward Stevenson. He was a short, little guy, scarcely five and one-half feet tall with a scar running the length of his neck and disappearing below a maroon, collarless, St. Andrew's football T-shirt. He was from upper New York and spoke Yankee through and through. In spite of his size, you could tell he was tough and that he only said things once. He began speaking before the door slid back into the jam.

"Gentlemen, you are now receiving your playbooks, a list of training regulations, and locker assignments. Coach Landers will be handing out gear following this meeting downstairs," he said, flying uninterrupted through his presentation.

"I want to introduce the other coaches," he said. Pointing, he continued. "Coach Spangler, Coach Bryson, Coach Winton, Colonel Shuford and Coach Hazelton."

They were all smiles and pride and hope were shown in their faces, anticipation in their hands and fire in their eyes, eyes which searched the room meticulously for their next star, their savior. Thirty minutes later, we were on the field starting calisthenics.

The initial hollering and clapping and growling caused you to feel strong and bold in this group but it didn't last long.

"Are you OK?" Sam asked, as we jogged side by side to the next training station.

"Good . . . I'm good . . . I'm OK," I said, wheezing.

"What about you? Are you OK?" I asked, my head bowed, my eyes on the ground.

"I should've worked out with you and Petey during the summer. I'm OK but it's killing me," he whispered.

"I told you to stop smoking," I said without conviction.

"Later," he said, "lecture me later," he said, his voice trailing away into silence.

The entire group was being pushed to their limit throughout the morning. It would be only days before the leader would emerge and I knew it wasn't going to be me. But I was intent on not backing off and I made my stand by ignoring my body and shutting off its need for rest and drink.

It is a law of the pack. One hesitation, one glance of fear detected by an older boy was as good as putting a target on your back. Once tagged, you would not survive the assigned identity. Not knowing what I was doing didn't help either. But I watched the obviously experienced boys and the gritting of teeth and bone and I imitated them. It was only the first hour and the weeding out had already begun.

"Over to the hill, gentlemen, get your butts over to the hill!" Winton yelled at our group.

We stumbled to the grass drills on a sloped thirty-foot hill with Colonel Shuford on top, looming like a giant.

"I'm dying," I said quietly to Sam. "I can't do this."

"Shut up," he said. "Don't stop. Just keep going," he said, gasping for air.

At the bottom of the hill, I lay in a muddy pile on my stomach. The thick, heavily dewed pasture grass stuck through my facemask and into my eyes. I strained my neck to look up this steep bank to see hand directions held against the hazy, Monteagle Mountain morning fog.

"Move it!" Colonel Shuford yelled, his hand pointing left, then right.

Barking and bellowing out his instructions, I reached my limit on Shuford's Hill. His voice was like an echo in my head. I could not hear him. I simply imitated the motion of the boys on my left and right. Causalities lay everywhere.

"You're in the trenches, gentlemen, and this is where you'll stay until you get it right!" he yelled.

Up we crawled and scratched, down we wheezed and moaned, our bodies going faster than we could control and sometimes finding ourselves at the whim of a centrifugal force, face down in the muddied field, clods of grass and dirt caked around our necks and facemasks. If there was a hell, this was it.

Herded in this pit together and knowing we weren't going anywhere, we aided one another, prodded the more out-of-shape ones, and gave encouragement to the disheartened and hopeless.

"C'mon, McNeal, get your ass up this hill!" the guy behind me yelled. I did not recognize him.

"C'mon, Flat Tire, c'mon, Flat Tire!" the President yelled.

Flat Tire was struggling, being a little overweight.

"If I beat anybody up this hill, I'll kick their ass! Adamsworth, you lazy piece of shit, move your lard!" someone yelled.

Whoever this boy was, he had been here on Shuford's Hill before.

Just at the moment I knew I could not go up this pinnacle one more time, our group was moved to the rope station. A brief reprieve descended.

As we moved to the next station covered with mud, we did not speak. Our movement was dictated by the swaying of the boy in the middle, left or right. We were reaching in silently to call on those spaces inside our hearts that gave each of us the strength to keep going. I was not going to be the first one to break.

Having had no clue into the murky waters of manhood, I could only figure that this was part of it, that pain was required, a way of transforming a little boy's salty tears into muscles of steely sweat by tests of physical endurance. I was willing to comply because momentarily, I believed this new journey was the beginning of becoming somebody, somebody other than who I thought was.

The morning came to an end with different locker assignments and the sound of a breathless, severed army staggering purposelessly to their bunkers. When I arrived at my locker, my name was scrawled on white athletic tape and taped to the top. McNeal I. Josh Beck, another new boy, was to my left.

"Are you OK?" Josh asked.

I did not answer.

"McNeal, are you OK?" he asked again.

"Yeah, I think so . . . Jesus," I said leaning over, placing my hands on my thighs, hanging my head.

"Fucking-a, man," he said, "I had no idea it was going to be like this."

"This is just the beginning. We have ten more days," I said.

"Fucking-a," he said, "I had no idea."

"Did you get by Shuford's Hill?" I asked.

"That wasn't my problem. I just rolled around half of the time. My problem was the gate. I rose up too soon one time and almost took my fucking nose off."

"You're still bleeding," I said, pointing to the wound.

"Man," Josh moaned, "that fucking gate killed me."

"Me, too. The same thing happened to me," I said. "Look at this," I said, pointing to the cut on my cheekbone. "I don't even know how I got this."

I met Josh for the first time at breakfast only hours before. He was from Athens, Georgia, and was a big boy. Dark-haired, burly and feisty, he didn't speak much longer, not having any energy left to carry on even the most meaningless of conversations.

As I was stripping, I saw the boy who pestered me during breakfast head down my row, displaying the same demeanor I endured at breakfast.

He looked at me slyly and said, "McNeal I, huh?"

"Yeah, that's right." I turned away from him again.

"I'm George Walker. I'm the prefect of St. George's."

"Oh shit," I said to myself, "a prefect."

I turned, held out my hand and we shook, our eyes locked. As our clasp pulled away, the conversation continued.

"Where are you from?" he asked.

"I'm from Monroe, North Carolina. Do you know where that is?" I asked.

"Nope," he replied.

"It doesn't matter. It's near Charlotte."

"Oh yeah, I know where that is," he said, starting to undress. I tried to pay as little attention to George as I could. I succeeded until he took off his shirt.

He resembled a small tank with biceps stretching from his brain to his fingertips. Still dripping with smelly sweat, his chest was massive and protruded from the rest of his body like a refrigerator door. I decided to change my mind and change it quickly.

"Well, this morning, I wasn't trying to be a smart ass. I thought you were trying to be an asshole or something. Not that you're an asshole. I just didn't know who you were," I said struggling to say the right thing.

"I guess some people think I am. I don't."

"Me neither, me neither. I just didn't know who you were," I said trying to save myself.

"I know what you were doing. That'll come in handy in some situations but not with me. Hey, I'm not going to give you a hard time unless you give me one."

"Not me, man. I just want to fit in and play football."

"You looked in shape this morning. You . . ."

"Me?" I interrupted. "You've got to be kidding. I worked my ass off all summer and it didn't do me a bit of good. I thought I was going to die," I said smiling.

"No, you did all right. No shit. What position are you going to play?"

"I don't know. I've never played."

"Never played? What did your old man do, make you?"

"No, I don't have a father. This was my mother's idea but I was OK with it. My brother was really the one who talked me into it," I said, pointing over to Sammy.

"That doesn't matter. You'll do fine. See you later."

"George, how many years have you been here?" I asked before he left.

"This is my fourth year. Why?"

"Nothing. Just wondering. See you later."

He trailed out of the sweat pen to the showers and although I didn't know it at the time, I had met a guardian of sorts. George Walker from Birmingham, Alabama.

The morning session ended with a two-mile run. The afternoon practice ended with a two-mile run, too. The rest of the day, concluding with a skull session at seven thirty that night, was a mere repetition of the morning. Although from deep within I felt that I had held up, I doubted I had the resilience to go the distance and secretly wanted nothing less than to go home.

I wrote my mother nearly everyday and called home collect every night. Only four days after my arrival and four long phone calls home, Mother wrote her first letter.

Dear Billy,

I had already written when you called tonight. I do hope you took my advice and found someone you could talk to about the way you feel. I know how you feel, son, and I sympathize with your feeling.

On the other hand, I don't think you would disagree when I say that I know you are in a position where you are now to receive a much better education than you would if you were here. We've been going over this before, and you've always ended up agreeing with me that your high school education is something that you do only once. People do make a lot of false starts in college and go back and do things over again, but it is seldom this way in high school. And in order to get into a good college, it is necessary to have a much better high school background than is possible to get in Monroe. Goodness knows, no one wishes more than I do that it were possible to get it here.

So, do use your head, because you have a good one, and realize that in order to make a good living for yourself and the family of your own that you will have someday, that education is an all-important part of your life right now and will be for the next six years.

No one can make you take what is offered to you, but I would remind you that what is best for you now is very closely connected to your future. In sending you to St. Andrew's I was doing what I spent many hours thinking about—and this was what was best for your future. I know we've disagreed about things a lot of times, but it has always been a consolation to me that you were man enough to come back and admit when you had been wrong and I had been right. And it takes a man to be able to admit he has been wrong.

Please believe me when I say that your being away is best for you, and do give things a chance. It's hard, I know, but so is living when we try to do what is right. No one ever said it would be easy. Just put your mind on your work and on football for the time being, and you will be surprised how fast time passes and how quickly we will be there to see you.

What you have to do is talk things out with someone and get down to work. Please, be fair to yourself, the school and to me and go on and do what must be done. I love you.

Mama

As the week unfolded, I wanted to run away but couldn't. I had no idea how to get back to North Carolina.

I would walk down to the front gates after lunch and sit. Just sit. I would watch and listen to each car as it was transformed from a silent speck of color to a loud bubble of steel and wonder where it was going and whether or not it was headed toward my home.

Phoning home every night, I ritually called Mother once more after supper.

"Operator, I'd like to place a collect call to Mrs. McNeal."

"What is the number you are dialing?"

"704-349-1257."

"Your name?"

"My name is Billy McNeal."

"Thank you. Please hold."

Please, Momma, oh please, be there and listen this time.

"I'm sorry, sir. The party will not accept the charges."

"What?" I asked.

"I'm sorry, sir. The party will not accept the charges."

For all of the confusion that was inherent in such perceived abandonment, I simply hung the phone up and returned to my room.

Time marched on and in two days or so, I found myself forgetting the boy who made those calls. Nevertheless, Mother felt a need to address what had happened by a letter that Sammy brought from the school store late one afternoon.

Dear Billy,

I hope by the time you get this that you will be feeling better. I am sorry that I had to deal with you sternly by not accepting the charges but I felt that I did what I had to do. So much of our happiness is within ourselves and unless we are willing to forget how unhappy we can be, we shouldn't expect happiness at home or away from home. There is a lot of man in the boy called Billy, and I hope to hear from the man soon.

Please feel free to call me whenever you think you need to but also bear in mind that there are a lot of things that we all want to do such as our trip up there and your and Sammy's trips home, and I still haven't taken my vacation and will need money for that when I do and telephone calls do cost money.

I promise you that I do not begrudge them one bit, but I would just like to be able to feel that all the decision-making, the hopes that I had about your education and the expense has been worth it. Just stop thinking about Billy for a while and what Billy wants and how Billy feels and put your mind to other things, and you will see how fast time goes.

Incidentally, I do know that love is a funny thing. Isn't it strange how happy it can make us and at the same time it is sad when we let it make us that way? It is the same way with life. We lose it when we live it only for ourselves and we regain it by living it, or parts of it, for others. Try to stop thinking of yourself and give a little thought to how others must feel. You'll feel better when you do.

Mama

But I could not. At sixteen, who else was there but me? Her words were of little consolation and once again, I felt like a prisoner on this mountain where home was replaced with unfamiliar hills and alien road signs. But the truth was that there was nothing about St. Andrew's that made me sad. I brought this sadness with me.

I walked down to the lake alone to sit on the dam, her letter in my back pocket. This unexceptional but natural setting was a special place for me from which the rising and setting of the sun could be seen in broken strands on the water's surface. From the grassy spot on which I consistently chose to sit, I could see the aged, red-worn barn off in the distance and patches of a sloping pasture that angled downward to the border of pine that lay along the school road. I carried a notebook with me and scrawled out another letter home with little hope of reprieve from Mother.

The first week was coming to an end. I survived the ordeal called early football and carved out a spot on the junior varsity team. George took it upon himself to talk with me on numerous occasions about being homesick and he seemed to genuinely understand.

While he eventually left me alone at meals, I'd catch a cautious glance from him as though he was issuing a warning about my behavior or my safety. The seniors zeroed in on a couple of guys who I did not know well. But they were not a part of our group in St. Patrick's and I took no initiative to interfere. Education through exclusion.

Letters from home zipped up to the mountain at a fierce rate during that period of time and none were able to soothe the discomfort that seemed to penetrate my every step. I was trying as best I could to push my anxiety away and ignore it.

CHAPTER 4

The Dailys

By the tenth day of school, I was acclimated to the schedule and had now belonged to a group of boys that made me feel like part of the crew. Classes were one day away from starting and all of the other boys from all over were beginning their pilgrimage back to St. Andrew's.

St. A. was a dormant heart whose blood was the breath of the boys who lived there. She lay asleep during the summer months. Awakened by the moans and cries of the first early morning football practice, she was brought back to life by the flood of bodies that arrived hourly the weekend before classes commenced.

We sat out at the quad like gargoyles as they came in car after car, filled with grandparents and freshly baked chocolate chip cookies. We ogled at their sisters and felt the heartbeat of St. A. pounding all around us. We pretended to be more than what we were.

While the faculty scooted here and there, hobnobbing with the coat and tied, we sat displaying our football wounds and lanced chests, courageous and fearless.

Mothers directed most of the traffic and fathers were lugging furniture and clothes bags like ants at a picnic. I spotted one boy crying and arguing, delivering a picayune plea to parents whose arms were folded and whose eyes were tilted upwards. He wasn't going anywhere today but to his dormitory room.

But the love that filled this space was working its magic, too. Held tightly to mothers' hearts and close to fathers' sides, boys walked among the pines to relive summer transgressions and start anew.

"What are you doing?" Sammy asked, stretching out on the bench beside me.

"Just watching," I said.

"Watkins and I are thinking about trying to change rooms, getting the room at the end of the hall."

"That'd be good," I said unconcerned.

Home was being carved out as brightly colored curtains were placed on the steel-framed windows that pushed out from each room. It was noisy and eventful, and at the same time, indelibly painful. It was the time of year that marked for parents the moment of greatest hope and prosperous futures and simultaneously, the moment of greatest separation for many boys.

We sat at the quad and watched the festivities as though we were beyond it. By this time those of us who were new were already old. Some of the green had ripened in us and what was left of traces of home had been torn from us by the rigor of our physical training. It was seen in our walk, in our entrances into rooms, and in our loudness. We were mistaken by new boys as old boys and that was not without its advantages.

As the carnival scene at the quad slowed with every passing minute, I strolled over to the cafeteria.

"Granny, do you have anything to eat?"

"Why, Billy McNeal, you know you're not supposed to be in here until five forty-five."

"I know but . . ."

"Step right over here. C'mon, step fast," she said.

I followed quickly behind her to the large oven that housed her homemade biscuits.

"Hold your hands out," she said smiling.

I cupped my hands and held them out as though I was taking communion.

"Boy, are they hot," I said, shifting the treasure from hand to hand.

"That's the way they're supposed to be," she said, patting me on the back. "Now, git, 'fore you git caught in here."

Like most of the new football boys, I gained Granny's affection and seeing her three times a day became uplifting.

As I came out of the cafeteria and began to round the corner, I saw this guy heading straight for me, going about twenty miles an hour, his arms swinging in stride like broken clock hands, just flying, his feet slapping the concrete. I froze to figure out whether to jump to the left or right to avoid being hit. As I leapt to the left side of the sidewalk, he slammed face-first into the cafeteria's gray, stucco wall.

He bounced off the wall, reeling about a foot backwards, adjusted the thick lenses of his huge glasses, and said, "Excuse me."

He walked off in the same suicidal march as he did before he hit the wall. I stood dumbfounded.

At that same moment, Macon Black arrived on the scene. Make was in his third year here, the epitome of the St. A. boy. I was fonder of Make than most of the boys I had met.

"Jesus, McNeal, he almost wiped you out!" Make said.

"What was that?" I asked completely bewildered.

"That, my man, was Pickens, a real a-hole. He's legally blind. He doesn't know you from that fucking bush. Man, I don't know how he gets around."

"Yeah, Make, but he hit the wall, man, he hit the wall and you're telling me he doesn't know the difference?"

"He's hit everything in this school. C'mon, I'll show you."

So, we followed Pickens into the administration building and watched him for a while. It was funny to the boy that was anxious to be liked by Macon Black, old boy, two-year letterman.

It was also sad and I felt compassion for the blind boy. But I did not allow myself to display it and I laughed along with my football friend. Perhaps Make felt the same way. I returned to my room and took a short nap.

The big moment finally ushered its way in and we began dressing in ties and blazers for our first official supper where all the priests, monks, faculty, coaches, students, and faculty children were to be present. It was a propitious time for school pride and dedication of individual heart and spirit to the goals of academic and athletic endeavors that lay ahead.

The cafeteria filled to the brim with brotherly warmth that momentarily soothed even the most homesick and dejected, and a barrage of maroon floated around each table. The banners above moved ever so slightly as the hot air filled this court of knights and their apprentices.

Father Henry stood at the helm. Father Bennigan, the prior, stood to his right. I scurried to an empty seat at the table with Father Hazelton who stood with his wife and two sons. Josh Beck, now dubbed "Bark" and Johnson Adamsworth, now dubbed "Limpy," stood there, also. There was one place left.

As quiet descended on this zealous herd, Father Henry began to speak.

"I want to begin by welcoming everyone to a new year. I hope you have found a seat at a table that should be headed by a faculty member or a senior. If not, gentlemen, would you please arrange yourselves appropriately," he said pausing.

Father Hazelton nodded, offering his approval of the seating at his table. I looked around. Sammy had his seat.

"Bless this food to our use and us to thy service, in Christ's name, Amen," Father Henry said.

"Amen," we echoed, as the underformer waiters came flying out of the cafeteria, the food trays held high, steam rising from the top. It was like the start of the Indianapolis 500, all bunched side-by-side together back in the serving line waiting for the starting word, "Amen."

We enjoyed a delicious, filling feast, gobbling down the first round. The conversations were brisk with more summer exploits and accomplishments and were they all true, I would have felt like a paralyzed slug having nothing to report. But I knew they were lies and I enjoyed them all the same. Instead, I laughed and held the napkin to my mouth to keep food from spilling on the table.

Father Hazelton was gracious and spoke principally of football.

"Billy, I thought you did well this week. Do you think you'll be ready next week?"

"Yes, sir, I will be. I'm ready to play."

"How is your mother? Have you spoken with her?" he asked.

"She's fine. I was calling her every night for a while but not anymore. I think she's fine."

"That's good," he said. "How do you think Sammy is doing?" he asked.

"He's doing great. He's better than me. I've never played before."

"You will do fine. I'm glad you decided to play. There are a lot of advantages to coming early. It seems you're already accustomed to the dailys."

Suddenly, I looked directly at him and he was looking straight at me, smiling.

"You will do fine," he said again.

I was moved by this fanfare, this camaraderie of maleness, my new home. Mystery meat, sweet tea, and fresh vegetables with Granny's home-cooked rolls adorned every table, as well as Mrs. Foster's homemade jellies.

Knowing Father Hazelton was at the head, I knew that I would get enough to eat and when the meal was over, I patted my stomach over and over, filled my cheeks with air, and smiled to show my appreciation to everyone at the table.

We were dismissed with a greater message of seriousness and call to arms. Tomorrow morning classes would begin. The wake-up call would sound at 6:15, breakfast by seven, chores and room inspection by seven forty-five, and required assembly at eight o'clock sharp. Being late to any function would be costly.

Being absent was not even considered.

CHAPTER 5

Monteagle Mountain

As a teenager home would be divided into two distinct memories: the home where I was born and the home where I was rescued.

The latter was an isolated, organized refuge where theology was a required subject. That made perfectly good sense to me, it being that St. Michael's monastery loomed over the whole campus like a parked cloud. It was like a tiny European city with God at its center, its inhabitants building their homes in circular fashion around it. The only difference was that our homes were dormitories.

The shadow of the cross that stood on top of the three-story, lodge-type building stretched across the entire upper lawn when the sun was just right. Its main door was actually no more ornamented than the screened, narrow, side entrance which would cause a visitor a moment of hesitation before choosing to enter because it was unceremoniously plain.

Eight white-trimmed windows, sought out by the climbing ivy below, stretched across the face of the second floor, topped by five double dormer windows on the third floor above. It was a commanding sight . . . secretive, dark, and yet, inviting.

Monteagle Mountain, on which the school was built, looked down on a world that seemed much more distant than the "less than an hour drive" it took to get anywhere else. For all of us, Monteagle Mountain was apart from the rest of the world, and it seemed the rest of the world knew nothing about our isolated existence. Our faulty perception compounded our isolation.

The winding drive up the mountain was always accompanied

by a feeling of withdrawal, like going out to sea or hiking through the wilderness and leaving behind familiar textures, everything that made me feel safe, whether they actually did or not.

From experience, I knew the number of curves going up the mountain to the lip of the Cumberland Plateau. Seventeen. The sight of the Holiday Inn on the left of Interstate 20 marked the top of the mountain and our entrance to the daily grind. The last ten minutes of the drive to the school entrance was always solemn, quiet and reflective.

The entrance, appearing suddenly on the right, was well-marked: St. Andrew's Episcopal School for Boys. From there, the road that led to the circular quadrangle was bordered on both sides by a two-foot rock wall. Beyond the knee-high wall on the right, wild pink and white dogwood trees were scattered across the open plot of land. The narrow, asphalt road was barely wide enough for two cars to pass. The speed limit sign read eight miles an hour. The odds of a head-on collision were remote.

Cameron Gymnasium and the adjacent track and football field could be seen off to the left down a short gravel road. It was the largest building on campus. For me, it was my monastery.

From this spot, I could barely make out the lake on the far side of the gym, behind and to the left. The border of swaying cattails gave it away. They would disappear when the fog, rising like steam from a simmering pot, would eclipse the entire lake. Immediately ahead on the left was the Headmaster's house whose front door opened onto the main road.

The first building on the right was the chapel. Its rust-colored, half cylinder-shaped tile roof blended in with the roofline of the administration building as if painted from a single horizontal stroke. The white crosses that formed the casing of the cafeteria windows blended with the worn, grayish, flat tile of the roof as though intended. Upon returning to campus, I felt like a medieval knight returning to my castle.

Dormitories surrounded the open quad area. St. Patrick's sat atop St. Dominic's beside the cafeteria. It had the advantage of having the woods in its back yard. St. Joseph's and St. George's dormitories were the furthest away, the home of the old boys. St. Alban's dormitory was the home of the smart boys and it sat to the left of the quad. Run-down St. David's and St. Paul's formed another two-story building, which completed the circular chain of residences.

The three-story academic building, to which all asphalt walkways led, could be viewed from virtually anywhere on campus. Built in 1905, it was coming to the end of its usefulness but maintained a historical respect. The basement and the third floor were blocked off. Rumors were always circulating about the walking dead who roamed those empty halls.

The entire campus lay nestled under an umbrella of pine, a sky of evergreen held up by massive, wooden veins spreading out in all directions around each tree. An air of majesty permeated this landscape. Surely, God did create this place. Although I had just arrived and was a new boy, I felt part of this landscape. St. Patrick's was my home and whether I realized it or not, St. A. was becoming my sanctuary.

Father Hazelton was my theology teacher and the school's chaplain. He was married, had two sons, and I took him to be an old man at thirty-five years old. I was told he had come from a church in Kentucky.

About five feet ten inches tall, one hundred and fifty-five pounds, he was robust and well built. He had straight, chestnut-colored hair, and we nicknamed him "Father Facetious" because he used the word so much. But he was a cheerful man who greeted everyone warmly, and I found myself immediately attracted to his self-confidence and intensity. Although I viewed myself as an academic weakling, I looked forward to each of his classes.

Father Hazelton was more than an Episcopal priest to me. He was real to me, although his stare did unnerve me from time to time. In his class, my main objective was to survive the game of school and hope that one day I would know as much as he did. I held no pretense of moving any closer to God. Though he was accepting and kind, I still felt emotionally and intellectually crippled.

One day, as we were examining the Holy Gospel according to John, I found myself, for the first time, deeply pondering his questions. I don't think that he really cared about convincing any of us to believe in God as much as he did teaching us how to make better choices for ourselves. I didn't really understand what was going on. I simply knew that I liked Father Facetious and that was enough.

He buzzed around the room, always waving his arms in the air like he was throwing a frisbee. His eyes would sometimes drift away upwards, but it didn't matter to me. He pranced around enthusiastically, patting us on the back like he knew us well. He made me laugh and feel no need to defend.

"So, gentlemen, there you are and you've been going on this trip for ten days, and you've about had it. You're out in some hilly country, and the driving has been smooth. You've been following the road map, but you're getting tired. It's turning dusk, the weather is changing for the worse, the highway doesn't appear to be marked, and you can't find it on the map. The road itself becomes rough. The tires are making a loud noise. And suddenly, up ahead, there is a looming hill. You're going about seventy-five miles per hour and as you start the climb, you realize that you've never seen the other side of this hill or this highway. What is it that gives you reason to believe that it's going to be there when you crest the top? How do you know that you're not going to drive off a cliff?"

There was a pause as he zeroed in.

"Nelson, what do you think?"

Nelson had been sitting there, head in his hands, elbows on the desk. He wasn't listening but he was thinking.

"Father, it's OK if you call me Flat Tire."

"Thank you, Flat Tire, but I prefer to call you Nelson. That is who you are to me. That may be different than who you are to your classmates. Is that all right with you?"

"I'm not sure what you meant but yes, sir, that's all right with me," Flat Tire replied.

Father Hazelton never called the boys by their nicknames. And we didn't call him by his. Flat Tire's thinking process wasn't very impressive.

"I don't know, Father. If I was getting scared, I guess I'd stop."

As Flat Tire fumbled for an answer, Father Facetious pressed on.

"But, Nelson, if you stopped, you would never get to the other side."

"But if I died, it wouldn't matter. There might be a cliff." Flat Tire was playing it safe.

"But how can you say you have lived until you have reached the other side?" Silence fell, our impatience for Flat Tire's reply increasing. Seconds ticked by as the priest leaned in, waiting, staying right in the boy's eyes.

"I don't know, Father. I don't know what to say."

"Neither did the Apostles, Nelson."

At his reply, I perked up. Everybody watched the exchange very carefully and anticipated Father Hazelton's next question. There was another pause as he drifted around our desks.

I never had a teacher like this before, a man who contemplated life, a thinker. My entire academic life up to this point had been under the instructional leadership of parrots.

Abruptly, he settled in front of me, grasping each side of my desk. Leaning over, hovering, he looked at me. His spectacular eyes stared a hole through me. He smiled without intimidating me.

"Billy, how do you know anything is on the other side? And if you believe it exists, although you've never seen it, then prove it's there."

"Oh, good Lord," I said to myself, "Please God, don't make me think. I don't even know where to start."

A lifetime passed. And for a child that is intellectually lame, that period of waiting is tortuous. Not receiving an answer, he moved on to another victim. Without bloodshed, we moved forward and the end of class ushered in a brief mental reprieve until the following day.

The rest of the day moved unceremoniously to supper where all faculty and students once again ate family-style. We stood silent, heads bowed, eight at each table headed by a faculty member or an upperclassman as Father Henry gave thanks.

"Bless this food to our use and us to thy service and make us ever mindful of the needs of others. In Christ's name we pray. Amen. Please be seated," he said, remaining standing to oversee the flock, his eyes scanning each table.

The cafeteria buzzed as the waiters came flying out of the kitchen, trays filled with Granny's cooking. Deals were struck for extra portions of meat or vegetable and God help every weak child there if it was the night of Granny's homemade rolls and preserves. Considering the prize, it was perfectly understandable to hear threats of the older boys, pocket change being flung from one table to another, and sometimes tears from the boys who lost out. I counted my blessings each time I ate more than one of her mouth-watering homemade biscuits.

After supper, every student marched to the silence of a two-hour mandatory study hall followed by a half-hour of free time before bedtime at 10:00. At lights-out, Speedy's forceful footsteps could be heard coming down the hallway checking each room. He walked unchallenged.

Mr. Spangler was an impartial but uncompromising man. He was demanding as a coach and feared as an authority figure but he grinned out of the corner of his mouth when he spoke, causing you to feel relaxed and safe.

When Mr. Spangler came down the hall, I whispered, "Goodnight, Speedy."

"Let's get some sleep, Mr. McNeal."

And from the other side of the hall, my twin brother would always make us laugh by blurting out, "What'd you say, Speedy?"

"I said to knock it off and get to sleep now." And yet I knew Speedy was smiling. He loved us boys.

Slowly, our hall became deathly quiet with occasional snoring or rustling of bed covers. In deep night I could hear a toilet flush or a creaking in the walls. But that night I did not sleep. Father Hazelton's words were eating at me, gnawing away at what defenses I could manage to conjure up.

I realized that it was not what he said that caused me to falter. It was that who and what I believed myself to be was not going to undergo the onslaught of close inspection and subsequent worthiness. I knew I would not measure up. I just didn't want anyone, much less him, to find out the truth. At some point, feeling vulnerable and weak, I nodded off.

CHAPTER 6

Father Henry

I reasoned that my fear could be resolved by running away. But considering the fact that I couldn't make enough geographical sense out of this place to run away without finding myself in Michigan somewhere and my mother's persistent attitude that I was going to make it hook or crook, I was stuck and I knew it. There wasn't much else to do but get in step and avoid being trampled.

I was completing my work job when Sammy brought Mother's letter.

"Letter for the homesick," he said, tossing the letter at my feet. "You better not forget the trashcan behind the desk. That's your job, too."

"How do you know?" I asked.

"Lassiter got two points for not doing it last week," he explained.

"I better not take any chances," I muttered.

September 5
Dear Billy,

I hope this wallet will be all right. The man I bought it from said that it would be a little fatter to carry in your hip pocket than the kind you usually carried.

I had two letters from you today and I was glad to read in one of them that you are feeling a little better. We have talked and talked this thing over, Billy, and I've written you each time to give you the advice that you say you would like to have, but evidently, you are not reading the letters. I am well aware how far you are from home, but I am also aware that it is the best place for you considering there are no schools in North Carolina that have a place for you and can offer you the education that St. Andrew's can. You are in complete misery because you choose to be. I have seen you in complete misery in Monroe, North Carolina, and no doubt I will see you that way again during the rest of our lives together.

So just come off the stuff about how badly you feel and how hard everything is and get down to work and do it right away. You have an opportunity, and I expect to see you feel a sense of obligation to this opportunity and to me. You should know by now that I have always tried to do what I thought was best for you, and I expect you to remember this in the future. So much for that. I hope from now on that both of our letters can be more pleasant.

Mama

I had no choice. I accepted my dilemma as best I could without revealing my intense, confused feelings, and sped onward. All of us were on our way through the first month and all of us had a fairly good idea where we stood in the herd.

The next morning I was completing my work job again.

"Man, I'm going to fail math," Bark said, waltzing into the room with Weaver. "I can't understand a goddamn thing in there."

I continued mopping the wooden floor.

"It's like Latin," he said.

"I don't have any doubt," I inserted, "that I'm going to fail. And I don't get it, either. Sammy's in this class where's he making straight A's and I'm in this class with a bunch of fucking Einsteins."

"Who's in there?" Weaver asked.

"Well, Miller's in there," I said. "Does that pretty much sum it up for you?"

"Jesus, you're in there with the scientists," he said.

"I'll never earn study-out going like this. I just don't get it," I said.

"Who's the teacher?" Bark asked.

"Dunston," I said.

"Well, shit, no wonder, McNeal. Dunston teaches the advanced classes," the President said.

"How do you know?" I asked.

"'Cause' I know," he said.

"Well, I'm not going to make it in there," I said.

Duck walked in.

"I saw you had mail so I brought it. Looks like another note from mommy," he said jokingly.

Having finished mopping, I sat down to read Mother's September 10th letter.

Dear Billy,

I enjoyed your letter that came today. I'm sorry about the B-team thing, but the way Sammy was talking about you yesterday, you will probably get to play a good bit. He told me you had done exceptionally well.

I'm glad to know you're working hard in your studies. Just don't let up. It's so easy to get behind when you do.

Eppie is fine. She's such a sweet girl, and she is very mature and understanding for a girl her age. But do as I said before. You should meet other girls. Just talking to a girl or dating one does not mean you're committed to her for the rest of her life. There is so much to be learned from others, and through knowing them and their feelings, we do learn to understand ourselves better. When you get right down to it, it is ourselves that we must learn to live with before we can possibly hope to have a lasting relationship with others.

I think I know better than anyone else how seriously you take things. You, Sammy, and I are all very much alike, perhaps because we've always been so close. And this serious side of all of us is good when we can use reasoning to work things out. It is a bit of a curse at times because when you are almost too sensitive in your relationship with others and it needs to be tempered with a little bit of the "what will be, will be" philosophy. After all, if, despite all we do, we cannot change a situation for the better, we should learn to accept it as it is. I'm not speaking of any particular situation . . . just life in general.

Keep working hard in your studies and on your football. You'll never regret an education, and you can never tell when someone might break a leg. Write to me soon.

Mama

I routinely folded the letter and was stuffing it into my pocket when George came in.

"What ya' got there?" George asked.

"Letter from my mother," I said, paying little attention to him.

"Does mommy miss you?" he asked.

"Don't think so. She's just afraid I'm going to run away," I said in a monotone voice as we both headed to assembly.

"Why would you do something like that?" he asked.

"The only reason I would is because I . . ."

"Cause' you're not happy, right? Jesus, McNeal, get real. Why do you think you were sent off?"

"It wasn't 'cause I wasn't happy back home."

"Oh no? Then why the fuck were you flunking out of school then? You go ahead and do something stupid and you'll regret it. You're better off here than back home. I know. I've been here for four years. I've been through all that shit. You think there weren't times when I wanted to go home? You think there aren't times when I still want to go home? But you don't get it, boy. You're gone from home and there ain't no going back. Once you're gone, McNeal, you're gone. The home you left ain't the same home you think you'd be going home to. You've been here almost a month, that's all. And that's all it takes. You can't go back home. It's time to wake up, dipwad."

He darted out of the room to catch up with Lizard.

I strolled into the assembly room and took my seat next to the President.

"Listen up and let's get started," Speedy said.

The hush began to die down, the attention focused on the man.

"I will need to see the following people at the end of lunch today: Johnson I, Haynes, Michaels, Benson, and Abernathy."

I turned to the President and whispered, "What did you do?"

"Goddamnit. I was late for English class yesterday," he said, putting his head in the palm of his hand, resting his elbow on the wooden armrest.

We all knew what Speedy meant. Licks. Licks for missing breakfast. Licks for failing to do your chores. Licks for being late to class.

The President returned to the room after lunch.

"Are you OK?" I asked.

"I don't give a fuck. He can't hurt me. I can take his goddamn licks."

"But are you OK?" I asked again.

"Hell, yes, I'm OK," he paused. "I'm OK. I'll make it."

Fall on the mountain is a glorious time and comes earlier than in the lowlands. As the leaves are stripped away, the tiled roofs of all of the school buildings become accentuated. The metallic dormitory window frames just below highlight the peeling paint and the need for renovation.

It is as though fall strips off nature's mask and we are able to see the school's evolution through time ever more clearly. Just as the trees are revealed by fall's chill, so are the things that they blanket.

"There have to be many boys who've passed through here," I thought to myself, "with promises they made to their parents that they could never possibly keep."

With the arrival of fall there are many signs that everyone has settled into the daily grind. There is less emotional upheaval, fewer pleading phone calls made to home, and a strong hint of academic seriousness that is even enjoyable and worthwhile. The grave reality is that there is nothing else to do.

But along with this settling, the minds begin to drift and the urge for mischief is strong. For the boys on the top floor of St. Patrick's, Halloween night was about to begin.

"Shut the fuck up, Flat Tire!" the President said.

"You shut up!" Flat Tire yelled back.

"Listen, if we're going to pull this off, we've got to stop making all this noise!" Yates said, revealing the flawless, ingenious, feeble plan.

"Look, there are ten of us," Bullet explained. "They can't possibly catch all of us. Nobody snitches! Nobody! We're going out the back, around the chapel and we'll attack from the Czar's house. Run like hell and get back here as quick as you can! You got it?"

Sammy was ready. "I ain't getting caught. I guarantee you that."

"Fucking-a," Limpy said, "if we get caught, our ass is grass. We better not waste any time."

Lookouts had been posted next to the bathroom windows and it wasn't long before the first warning came.

"Speedy's coming!"

Everyone bolted back to his room, trampling anyone who got in the way. The fear was staggering, our insides about to explode.

"Shhh. Don't move," the President said.

Like corpses, we stood. But tonight Speedy never arrived.

Hatch was at the lookout post. Suddenly, he whispered loudly, "It wasn't him. It's OK!"

"Bullshit, Hatch! Fucking idiot! You can't tell who's going or coming!" Frankie argued.

"Fuck you, Frankie. You don't know nothin'. I know what I saw!"

"If I get caught, Hatch, I'm going to kick your ass," Frankie argued.

"Then stay here, you pussy! You're too afraid, anyway!"

"If y'all don't shut up, we ain't ever going to get out of the dorm," Duck said, having joined us from St. Joseph's dormitory, doing what he could to get everyone settled down.

The President was irrepressibly mischievous with a million tricks up his sleeve. Although his gall surpassed my own, I, too, was through playing by the rules. I rationalized that I had been stuck here against my wishes. So, I justified joining this adventure. It was too intoxicating to pass up.

Off we tiptoed with sheets over our heads in nothing but our underwear and tennis shoes. We were an untouchable band of misfits about to rape, pillage, and plunder this school until it buckled under our collective power.

"Shhh! Quiet!" Sammy said.

"Hey, dumb ass," Watkins said, helping Sammy tweak his disguise, "your sheet's dragging. Better pull it up or you'll fall."

We headed down the left stairwell, out the back door, and assembled at the other end where we were partially shadowed by tall nellie foster bushes. The air was cold and swirled around our legs causing all of us to rush the onslaught prematurely.

A little movement started at the front of the pack, some pushing began, and before we knew it, like dominoes, we were airborne.

We tore around the chapel screaming, dead pine needles flying up everywhere underneath our shoes, sheets flapping.

"Boo! Boo!" rang everywhere, ghosts attacking the dormitories from every side.

"Boo! Boo!" we yelled and screamed, sheets flying in the wind, arms waving madly, lights being turned on inside dormitory rooms and faculty apartments.

Trouble was seeking to know itself. We circled St. David's, made our way up and behind St. Henry's jumping up and down maniacally!

"Boo! Boo!" we screamed.

As we headed by the front of Hughston Hall to attack St. Joseph's and St. George's, my heart stopped.

I caught the sight of Mr. Van Broughton out of the right corner of my eye, and I reeled around to escape along the same route that this unfruitful disaster began. Safety was not to be found this night.

We tore this way, then that, the well-formed plan disrupting into chaos. Each of us fought the crowd of ghosts to scamper back to our rooms without being identified.

Our tribe reached our rooms, stashed our sheets, and I covered my head with my pillow for I knew deep down inside that it was only a matter of time now.

"Oh shit," the President said, hiding in his blanket as best he could, "we fucked up now. Prepare to get NNOKIed."

"That's right," I said, "we fucked up big time."

When the hall lights were switched on, I was not surprised and I could hear Speedy's footsteps.

"Gentlemen, get out here right now."

And we did, the entire hall population assembling fearfully on the cold floor along the wall.

"I'm only going to ask one time and I better get what I'm looking for. Any of you that had something to do with this ghost run, get your butts down to the quad right now. You have two minutes and two minutes only."

Speedy was focused.

"Pack it good," Bullet said as we exited our rooms and looked gloomily at one another.

I put on the thickest pair of corduroy pants I had and off I went to gather with the condemned.

Four or five were already there. When everyone finally assembled, there were ten. No one dared not to show up. Such cowardice would hunt you down in so many unsuspected ways and would last far longer than what was about to occur.

We were lined up in a single file and without discussion, the paddling began. Three licks apiece. It may just as well have been ten. It wouldn't have mattered to me. My turn came quickly.

"Bend over, Mr. McNeal," Speedy said.

I knew not to ask for mercy. There were tears in my eyes before the first swat hit me. I cringed and buckled, simultaneously holding on to the back of my knees in order to keep my balance. The second lick struck ruthlessly below the middle of my buttocks and what grace I had in accepting this punishment vanished.

The third lick hit me with such force that I was unable to prevent my body from lurching forward where I went to the asphalt on my hands and knees. I rose, kneeling, rocking and sobbing, my hands folded in my lap and my head bowed.

"Shit," rose from my throat.

"Bend over again, McNeal, and watch your mouth this time."

"Please, Speedy, don't . . ."

"Bend over!" he said.

The blow sent me to my knees again.

I struggled to get my legs outstretched so that I could sit with my fanny on the cold asphalt. I began inching forward, crawling in this position, dragging my ass along.

It was the only thing that relieved me of the pain. After ten or twelve feet of this, I was sternly ordered back to my room.

I lay in the bottom bunk on my stomach feeling sick and injured.

"That SOB didn't hurt me at all," the President said.

"You're lying and you know it," I said, angrily. "But you're not alone. God, he killed me," I said.

In his raspy, country, South Carolina accent, the President went on about his revenge. He was stoic about the pain. He did the best he could to pretend that it didn't bother him.

For me, I knew that it was the last time that I would attempt anything like that again. Or so I thought.

"Big time last night, McNeal. I heard you got it," George said as we stood in the breakfast line. I was embarrassed but proud.

"Yep, big time. It was fun but Speedy NNOKIed us good. I wish I hadn't done it. I bet it took him less than ten seconds to paddle all of us."

"If you do things like that, you'll hurt your chances of making it here. I'm not trying to be your daddy. You could be a prefect if you wanted but not if you keep going in this direction. I'm just giving you some free advice. You can take it or leave it."

"I'll take it," I said.

I learned my lesson but did not learn it well enough. It could not have been more than two weeks later, just prior to the annual

Parents Weekend, when I found myself in the same situation again. I was in the mood for pushing the boundaries a little further out, giving the cow a larger pasture to graze. I was a slow learner.

This magical night was headed for trouble and taking me with it.

Mr. Douglas, the study hall master, was reigning tonight with unusual force and several boys had already been sent to see Speedy.

"Supervised study hall sucks," Jew-Jew said during break.

"I'm about to lose my mind sitting up there," Dumbrowsky complained. "What the fuck do they want?"

"We'll get out of here next time," Limpy moaned. "Big Dave, Bullet . . . those guys always have study out."

"I think that, unlike you," Duck said, "they actually study."

"Come to think about it, Duck, I really didn't like fucking your mother that much, but if . . ."

"Up yours, Limpy, or whatever the fuck they call you," Duck said.

"Is the door to the fire escape open?" I asked.

"All of the time," Wreck squeaked.

His voice was always broken, his intonation up and down, like something was stuck in his throat.

"You can't go down the fire escape," Maguire said adamantly.

"Why not?" I asked. "Maybe I could."

"Yeah, maybe I could blow up Scabie's history class but I ain't going to," Maguire said.

"Who's Scabie?" Wreck asked.

"Chamberlain, dumb ass!" Maguire replied.

"Did you hear what happened yesterday?" Bark asked. "Yesterday, stupid Limpy was in his class and asked to go to the bathroom. Instead, he went downstairs and started shaking the steam pipes that run up the wall to his room. Man, it was hilarious! Scabie came screaming down the stairs yelling, 'Damnit to hell! Damnit to hell! Who's shaking my pipes?' and Limpy ran to the other end, went up the stairs about the same time Scabie was coming down, and ran down the hall to class and was in his seat before Scabie got back. Man, that was funny!"

"Won't be funny if you get caught," Wreck squeaked again.

Jew-Jew couldn't hold back. "Can't you talk right? What's in your throat that makes you . . ."

"Shut up. Leave him alone," Flat Tire said.

The first bell rang and we were on our way back up the stairs. Together, we dragged our feet and went saintly marching on to war.

I plotted an escape route with the help of the crew. When Douglas turned his head, I rolled from my desk to the floor where I froze on my hands and knees. Douglas was too far away to see me.

Only upon being given the signal from each of my cohorts in crime would I inch forward. But forward, I moved, guided by whispers.

"Go!"

"Freeze!"

"Low!"

Finally, I was at the exit. All I had to do was wait. I remained huddled and completely hidden behind Limpy's desk. Limpy did all he could to spread out so as to cover me up as much as possible. And when the time came, I was ready.

"Out!" Limpy coughed.

And out I went. It was so fast, so ingenious, and so stupid. I was stealthily inching my way down the iron steps when I heard his dreaded voice.

"Who's that up there?" he sternly yelled. "Get down here right now!" He just happened to be walking down to the gym.

I began to cry. I knew what this meant.

"Please, Father Henry, please let me go," I pleaded. "I promise, Father, if you'll let me go, I promise I won't do another thing wrong for the rest of my time here at school. I'll never do anything wrong again. Please, Father. Don't paddle me. I mean it, I swear," I said, head bowed, sobbing.

He looked at me and paused. He was not angry but he was not indifferent. He simply put his hand on my left shoulder, and asked, "Mr. McNeal, look at me. I have one question for you. Are you a man of your word?"

Looking in his eyes, I did not hesitate. "Yes, Father, I am."

"Mr. McNeal, listen carefully to my question again. Are you a man of your word?"

"Yes, sir, I am," I said, wiping the snot dripping from my nose.

"See to it, Billy. Don't waste your time here. I'll speak with Mr. Douglas later. Wait in Father Chamberlain's room until the break and then go back to study hall."

"OK, Father." He started to walk away in the darkness toward the gym. "Father?" I said.

"Yes?"

"Thank you. Thank you very much."

"Remember what you said, Mr. McNeal. I expect you to keep your agreements with me."

"Absolutely, sir. I will, Father, I will." He disappeared into the dark between the two buildings.

I crept into Father Chamberlain's empty classroom unnoticed and waited patiently until the moment I could describe my parole hearing to the crew.

I had escaped death. I was certain I had snookered my way out.

CHAPTER 7

Homecoming

One night, a week following the event, Sammy came by my room before lights-out.

"Has Mom called?" he asked.

"Nope, why would she?" I said, without looking at him.

"Are you going to call her?" he asked.

"Nope," I said.

"Why not?" he asked.

"Because," I said. "If you want to speak to her, then you call her."

Tess of the D'Urbervilles fell to the floor.

"I hate that fucking book," he said.

"Me, too," I said, as I picked it up and continued to read.

"What's wrong with you?" he asked.

"Nothing," I said.

Raising his voice, he replied, "Then why are you . . ."

"Look, if you want, call her yourself. I've got to get this done or Jordan is going to kill me tomorrow."

"I think he's pretty OK, if you ask me," he said.

I smiled and leaned back in my chair.

"Yesterday," I continued, "he came up to my desk, looking right at me, and got about a foot from my eyes, and said, 'And what would the essence of that word suggest, Mr. Larue?' Well, Duck was nodding off and never heard him. He just kept looking at me while he was asking Duck the question. I got ready to say something and he put his finger up to his mouth so I'd know not to say anything and he went on over to Duck's desk. Man, everybody started laughing."

"So, when are you going to call Mom?"

"I'm not," I said interrupting him, "I'm not."

"Fine," he said, "I'll call her."

"You do that. Listen," I said, "I want to ask you something."

"No, you're not going to ask me anything. I'm not going to talk about it. Your problem is you take things personally and you're too sensitive, you let things get to you. Just forget about it."

"That might be . . ."

"Shut up," he said, changing the subject, "just shut up."

I raised my eyes and studied my brother. He wore his secret better than I, never gliding too far left or right. He bore the task of soaring above, the dutiful one, the flyer. I often found myself envying him, his stoicism, his ability to deflect, and wished I were as strong.

Where I lacked his ability to empty himself of the pain and speak from the void, he lacked emotional honesty and vulnerability. Where he sought survival, I sought release.

The Parents' Weekend, for which I had once so desperately longed, suddenly mattered little to me. It was Friday afternoon.

"Your mom's waiting for you and Sammy up at the dormitory," Weaver said.

"Thanks, "I said.

Sammy caught up with me on the walk from the gym.

"Have you seen Mother?"

"Nope," I said, "and I'm not sure I want to. I failed two tests this morning and got extra work detail of mopping floors in the old school building because P.W. said he found a match under my desk. Of course, it was the President's, but I didn't say anything. So I haven't exactly had a good day so far."

"No sweat," he said, "you've got to . . ."

"There's Mother," I interrupted.

We walked shoulder to shoulder towards her.

"Hello, boys," she smiled, as she hugged us separately. "What are your schedules this afternoon? We are going to join the Campbells and Abernathys for dinner tonight, and I need to go back to the hotel to get ready."

She picked up as though we had never left.

"Why don't you come back for us at about six o'clock?" Sammy asked, all of us heading towards St. Patrick's.

She followed us to our rooms to verify for herself the cleanliness and order she felt so necessary. There were no details of campus life left untouched.

"Billy, I ran into Mr. Jordan earlier and he told me that you were playing varsity now."

"Mom, he's doing really good," Sammy pitched in.

"Really well, Billy, really well," Mother affirmed.

"To be honest," I said, "I'm not that good. I'm doing the best I can. I'm starting tomorrow in the game. I'm first-string wingback."

"Honey, that's great. I'm so proud of you. What time is the game? Do we have time before the game to go into town for lunch?" she asked.

"Not exactly," I explained. "We've won our first three games and they've all been away games. So, Coach Stevenson came up with this idea that we would act like it's an away game, so, we're leaving on the bus at ten o'clock and we'll come back about twelve to get ready for the game."

"How clever," Mother said suspiciously.

The evening came and went uneventfully. I felt unexpectedly indifferent to her visit.

As the car circled around the quad to stop, Sammy jumped out yelling, "See you tomorrow. I promised Duck I'd meet him at the lounge."

My mother and I were alone.

"How is school going, Billy? Are you studying like you should?"

"I'm fine. I'll be OK," I said.

"I spoke to Father Hazelton. He said that he enjoys having you in class but feels like, at times, you are somewhere else," she said, her eyes focused on my response.

"I'm OK. Just takes some time to get used to everything," I said.

"Is there anything you need to talk about?" she inquired.

"No, I'm fine," I replied. I had no intention of speaking about my feelings.

That midmorning, after our training meal and skull session in the gym, we loaded up on the bus with all of our equipment and headed down the mountain. It was the biggest game of the year and was held in front of the largest crowd of the year.

It was also the biggest disaster of the year. In front of our loved ones who trekked hundreds of miles, we were drummed forty-six to seven by our archenemies, the Gimps.

Every SMA cadet marched in to view the slaughter and marched out laughing and jeering. We were humiliated beyond recognition and I chose to spend the remainder of the afternoon and early evening by myself in my room. So much for the home-game-away-game plan.

When I finally joined Mother and Sammy to leave for supper, I was embarrassed and hurt, my pride injured and shaken.

"Man, they kicked your ass," Sammy said.

"So, you noticed, huh?" I said pushing him but smiling.

"Yeah, but you scored a touchdown," he said.

"So what? Big deal. We got our ass kicked," I said.

"I got a picture of you catching the ball. I knew they were going to throw it to you."

"Well, do what you want with it. I don't care. I just want to pretend this never happened," I said.

Mother and I talked at length about my academics and it was all the more plain to me that she, too, had gone about altering her life to make way for the changes she was encountering.

In such little time, the world as we knew it had been transformed and rearranged. This long awaited pleasure cruise turned shipwreck came to an end. By Sunday morning I couldn't wait for her to leave.

The hundred or more separate families that had invaded the mountain were recapitulating their steps and the ritual scene I witnessed only two months before was being carried out again as departure was underway. By late afternoon, the sounds of engines in reverse and loud goodbyes trailed off and quiet returned to the quad and the pines. The banners were still in the cafeteria.

A week later, Mother wrote.

Dearest Billy,

I know you are spending a lot of time thinking about coming home, but you must stay on your work. The time will pass, as I told you it would before, and it will be so much nicer coming home for a rest knowing that you have left your work in good order when you do leave.

Do get your face in shape. I sent the medicine and things, and if you will just attend to it three times daily (not once and not twice, but three times daily) it should be cleared up by the time you come home. Don't drink any cokes or eat any chocolate.

Tater Edwards is leaving for Camden Military Academy this Sunday. He got his first report card from Monroe High, and he had four F's. Keep your mind on your work, too. I went to the cemetery yesterday and fixed new flowers. You can change them if you want to when you come home, but they will still be pretty.

Mama

That afternoon I went on a walk to the backside of the cemetery behind the monastery where I sometimes walked for some peace and quiet. This time, I studied the gravesites.

In 1912, Jack Rutherford, an eighteen-year-old student at St. Andrew's, died of typhoid fever and became the first of about thirty persons to be buried there. Three years later, Jennie Hennington, was the first of several matrons of St. Andrew's to be buried in the cemetery. In 1954, another matron, Lillian Killabrew, was buried there, and in 1964, Elizabeth Hunziker followed her footsteps.

Albert Hunziker, Elizabeth's husband, was buried next to her. Since then four of their children, who were students at St. Andrew's, were buried near their parents. One of the children, Andrew, gave some land behind the monastery to the school on which the cemetery is located. Besides Ricky Neely, a bookkeeper at St. Andrew's and Ellen and George Wilson, a business manager's parents, there are several students buried there. Joseph Mulhaney, a day student, was buried there in 1928, after being murdered by a neighbor following an argument. In 1933 Douglas Caldwell, a former student, was buried there upon request.

Mr. Jimmy Stackey was buried there in 1926. He ran the post office for many, many years and the post office became known as Stackey's following his death.

Father Erskine Wallace, who was for years the school's business manager, was buried in 1949. His wife, Linda, was buried there in 1964.

Most recently buried in St. Michael's Cemetery were Mr. Morris Allison, whose name was given to the gymnasium, and Mr. Paul "Sunrise" Stilwell. Sunrise was a former student and was a thoroughbred mountain man. He was a legend of the school.

Somewhere in that brief walk and tour of the dead at St. Michael's, I buried something, too. Perhaps it was part of the little boy in me, part of the gullibility, and part of my innocence.

I imagined what my tomb would be like and what words would be etched upon my slab of dull, gray granite. As the purple procession approached with the preceding incense and cross-bearing acolyte, what would they say when they gathered at my resting spot?

I wondered if I would matter at all.

CHAPTER 8

Monteagle Melancholy

After crying on the fire escape that night in 1967, I had no reason to cry again that year. I kept my promise to Father Henry and I worked diligently to get out of required study hall. I was studying in my room before we left for Thanksgiving break and was enjoying the freedom that came with it.

I hid junk food under a small box that I kept at my feet and as soon as the prefect walked by, I munched on penny candy and chocolate and sipped sodas. Eating food during room study would land me back in supervised study and I had no intention of returning there. I was vigilant in hiding my treasure.

We had but one sad event that occurred on campus that outweighed many others of lesser importance. It was the first snow of the year in the early part of December 1967.

On that particular morning, the cold crept quickly up the slopes of Monteagle Mountain and delivered a shivering, early wake-up call to the sleepy inhabitants.

When I arrived at the morning assembly, the talk was fast-paced and I surmised that for reason of tradition, we were given a free day on the very first snow of the year, which was being anticipated. While the snow had not arrived yet, the ice was forming solidly on the rooftops, walkways, and pine limbs. The trees, now drooped and bent-over, were like a line of actors and actresses accepting an encore following their performance before an appreciative audience, with hands held tightly. We knew the snow was coming.

At break, we discovered that the snow had still not started and we were growing impatient. No sooner had I exited the classroom door than the whispering voices could be heard.

"Pickens on the side door! Pickens on the side door!"

A quiet wave of warning spread everywhere.

Everyone hustled out the side door whose doorsteps were frozen solid with a sheet of fresh winter ice. A semi-circle was formed around the entrance and was being hushed to complete silence by several sixth formers as someone propped open the door. I saw Pickens, the blind boy, coming at the other end of the hall.

"Watch him," Make said. "I got money he's never going to see it."

"Oh shit," Jew-Jew laughed, "he's going to bust."

Here Pickens came, head tilted to the side, his one good eye pinned to the ground in front of him, bouncing at breakneck speed toward this exit. I said nothing but watched cruelly as did my friends.

When Pickens hit the first step, his feet immediately rose vertically above his head, books and papers flying symmetrically into the crowd. He instinctively tried to use his hands to cushion the fall that was to no avail. His back and side landed on the third or fourth step as the crowd flew away laughing and joking.

The blind boy was on his stomach now in the icy dirt, motionless.

Knowing that we would be disciplined for taking part in such a senseless prank, we scattered quickly. As I turned to see him one more time, it began to snow and the boys' cries of joy could be heard from all directions of campus life. I wanted to help but knew the consequences outweighed my weak resolve.

It was the last time I saw Pickens. He was removed from school with a broken wrist and dislocated hip and we would never hear from him again. For me, he was the first true casualty of the year.

Shortly after the turn of December, I was hit with another episode of depression that centered on the death of my stepfather to which I responded by writing home. My ambivalent feelings about him could not openly be discussed with anyone, so I naturally disguised my true feelings and would point to his death as the cause of my upset and confusion.

It was a protective smokescreen to cloak deeper and darker angers

I maintained alongside the expected need to preserve the image of a
loving and responsible father. Nonetheless, it was an attempt, as best
as I could, to try and speak out. Nobody knew any different.

Dearest Billy,

I hope by the time you get this that you are feeling
better. I understand your feelings, honey. These things always
come back to us every now and then, and it is hard to
understand. I couldn't possibly tell you how it happened. I
really don't think I ever bothered to find out because all one
can do about something like that is to speculate. The one
fact remains after all the guessing is done is that it happened
and all the guessing in the world will not change this. And
those who are left just have to keep going and remembering
preferably the good things and the good times that were
had before it happened. But so many times when it does
come back and we remember and it makes us sad, we cry,
but we're crying for ourselves . . . out of loneliness and out
of wishing for something or someone that is gone.

Grief is a selfish thing. All this doesn't make us feel any
better, and it's best to go ahead and cry when you feel like it
and get it out of your system. I always wish that I could be
with you when you feel this way; I also wish that you could
be with me when I feel this way. But I know that Father
Hazelton is there and that you trust and respect him and
that you do have him to talk to when you need someone.
We can talk about it when you come home.

Billy, your grades really are not what they should be.
I'm not saying that it's easy, but I don't feel that you are
spending enough time with your books working on your
lessons. You still have a little over a week before you come
home, so please do get down to doing some hard and
concentrated work.

Mama

Christmas came and went with little time spent with Mother. I could not wait to get back to St. Andrew's.

As soon as we returned from the Christmas break, I was immersed in sports again and had little time for anything besides basketball and my studies. A boring, cold, typical January mountain Saturday, Make and I hitched into town, browsed through the books at the university bookstore, and made a general nuisance of ourselves.

"Hey, have you ever seen old man Dawson?" Make asked.

"Who's he?"

"You've never seen him?"

"I've never even heard of him."

"Well, man, you're in for a real treat. Let's go."

We scooted out of the bookstore entrance and headed down to the grocery store on the main highway, talking about school, and giving a couple of Gimps the finger as we passed by.

"This guy, Dawson, hangs out down at the store every Saturday and you're going to shit when you see him."

"Why? What's wrong with him?"

"I ain't telling. You'll have to wait and see. Man, you're not going to believe it."

When we got there I didn't spot anyone or anything unusual, but Make identified his truck. As we were crossing the street, a strange-looking farmer in overalls and a dark flannel shirt strutted out of the store and flopped down on one of several benches there in front of the store drinking an RC and eating a moon pie.

"That's him, Billy. Look."

"What's that between his legs? Is he hiding his groceries in his pants?"

"No, man, those are his nuts! Shhh! Shhh! Don't say anything. Let's go inside, get something to eat, and come back out on the other bench."

"You're bullshitting me. Those ain't his nuts."

"No shit, man, I ain't kidding."

When we hit the edge of the gravel parking lot, we grew quiet and it was everything I could do to keep from staring. When we exited the store with candy bars and cokes, we sat down on another bench just up from him and waited.

Wadding up the moon pie wrapper and throwing it in the trashcan, he placed his hands on knees to rise. Moaning, he stood slowly and began making his way back across the street in the direction of the seed and feed store, as if a pillow was dangling back and forth between his legs.

Make was giggling.

"There you go, McNeal. The worst case of testical elephantitis in history. Nuts are as big as summer cantaloupes. Goddamn, what a man!"

"Those things in his britches are his nuts?"

"Hell, yes! Everybody knows about him. But he doesn't care. He walks around with them anyway."

"I don't believe . . ."

"Well, what you got to do to believe it, go up and stroke one of them? I promise you, those are his nuts," he insisted.

""How does he even walk?"

"Man, that'd be the least of my problems."

"That's really something. And I thought going into town today would be a waste of time. I appreciate you showing me . . . his, uh, nuts."

We laughed, finished our snacks and got on the road to back to school.

Mother felt a need to address our behavior during Christmas vacation and her letter arrived on Monday, two days later.

———————

Dear Sammy and Billy,

I'm sorry you had such a rough trip back, but it was just one of those things that couldn't be helped. I hope by the time you get this you will have rested enough that you are feeling better. You must have been worn out Thursday. Needless to say, I was also feeling much better today.

Sammy, did you get your hat? I thought maybe you might have forgotten it since I didn't see how you could have had it in your luggage without having smashed it.

Billy, please don't plan on making any phone calls any time soon unless you have the money to pay for them. The phone bill looks like the national debt.

Please remember to write thank-you's to folks who gave you such nice gifts. Don't forget Aunt Mildred, Mattie, Aunt Winnie, and Uncle Ed and all the rest.

I hope you two get settled down. I know you're getting older and growing up, which is to be expected, but when you're away for a few months and then come home wild as bucks I'm not able to catch up with you long enough to even talk over things that I would like to discuss with you. And don't forget what I said about the smoking and drinking. Any of that except when you're with me is out, and if you find it necessary to go back on your word where this is concerned, you will be needing skate keys this summer instead of automobile keys and this is a promise.

I love you both very much and I miss you. I'll send you a few things to eat in the next week or two when I get time to get them together. Please work hard in your studies and write when you have time.

Mama

I once again found myself enjoying the rigid schedule and the constant expectations. I labored in class, and, had it not been for math, I would have been a very reliable student. While I was certainly not an honor student, I was taking pride in keeping up and I looked forward to learning more.

I read constantly and discovered a love for literature, particularly French literature. I took three squares a day, rising at six fifteen and falling fast asleep at ten o'clock at night. I was in the groove.

Mother couldn't help but respond to my letter of apology.

Billy,

I do understand. It's time you were beginning to get out on your own, and there's no reason why you should be expected to sit at home with me all the time. My gripe was that you spent your time with other people without considering the inconvenience it might cause me and without doing the things I asked you to do at home before you went out. Goodness knows, I know how you feel. I've felt that way a hundred times, and it's a good feeling. But I wish you would consider that there are other people in the world beside yourself and do the things I've asked you to do. I don't see how you can "save every cent you can" if you don't have anything to save. You spent your money as you pleased, so you shouldn't have expected to have any when you got back to school. I mean, use a little common sense; if you spend all you have, how in heaven's name can you save any? If you want to be "Easy Come, Easy Go," learn to live with the consequences. All of that is behind us now, but I hope you learned a lesson from it. Don't go into a tizzy about the weekend thing. Just do as I asked you to do and think about it. In the meantime, if I find the money tree, I'll send you a limb.

Mama

After two weeks back on the mountain, I was called into the guidance office.

"Have a seat, Sammy," Mrs. Graham, the counselor, said.

"Thank you," I replied, worried. I knew I wasn't being called in here to play scrabble.

"Sammy, I've asked you to come in today to talk about your math grade. You're not doing very well and I'm worried about whether or not you're going to pass."

"Mrs. Graham, I'm not Sammy. I'm Billy."

"You're not Sammy?" She was definitely puzzled.

"No, ma'am."

"Are you sure?"

"Yes, ma'am."

"Aren't you in Father Dunston's geometry class?"

"Yes, ma'am, I am."

"What class is Sammy in?"

"Sammy's in Mr. Spangler's class."

"I think we have made a big mistake. Sammy is supposed to be in Father Dunston's class and you are supposed to be in Mr. Spangler's."

"Well, Mrs. Graham, I believe that, too. I'm flunking and Sammy's making A's. He has always been better in math than me and I don't understand a word Father Dunston says anyway."

"OK, Billy, I'll see if I can get this straightened out. I'll speak with you tomorrow."

"OK," I said, "Thank you."

I didn't know what else to say.

"Thank you, Billy. I am very sorry about the mistake."

"That's all right," I said.

Father Dunston had stopped worrying about me a long time ago and I could not blame him. I wanted to pretend that I would recover, but I knew differently. I wasn't going to pass.

The next day, I was informed that my geometry class and my brother's geometry class were being switched. Mr. Spangler was now my math teacher.

Six weeks later, I jumped to an eighty-three and Sammy's grade plummeted to seventy-six. I discovered there were boys in the class who were dumber than me. Maybe Father Dunston had taught me something after all. I was certainly willing to pretend.

Suddenly, I was good at geometry and I was elated.

But winter is a time for hibernation on the mountain, and we did little else but study and watch college basketball in the lounge. We were frequently snowed in and there was little chance of getting out even if you wanted to go into town.

If there was no snow, there was still nothing to do in town besides see a movie and walk around the University of the South. Over the course of these sequestered months, I had little contact with home.

As basketball came to a close and baseball sign-ups were posted on the locker room doors, hints of the changing season came intermittently with occasional glimpses of sunshine and warmer temperatures.

Springtime came slowly on the mountain and we prepared to see home once again. Easter break and baseball were just around the bend.

CHAPTER 9

The Morning Watch

"What time do we go?" the President asked as lights-out approached.

"Says here two forty-five," I said.

"Morning? Two forty-five in the morning?" he asked.

"Yep, that's what it says here."

"Jesus, maybe we'll get to sleep in."

"Nope, that's not what it says here. We have to be at assembly at seven thirty," I said.

"I don't get it." the President asked, "Why do we have to go watch the chapel? If Jesus is supposed to be buried there, why do we have to watch it?"

"Get your lights out!" M.B., our prefect, yelled.

"I don't think he's buried there. It's just pretend," I said. "We just go in and watch it to make sure that nothing happens to it, I guess."

"How long do we have to stay?" he asked.

"Fifteen minutes. Make and Bullet are coming in after us."

"Who's in front of us?"

"Let's see . . . looks like Droo and Robo I."

"Who's the master of the day?"

"Looks like Winton is," I said.

"Shut up, BillyBob," M.B. said, "and go to sleep."

"Hey, M.B.," I asked, "who's in charge of waking us up?"

"You are, dipwad, and don't be late," he said.

"Thanks for your help, Mr. Prefect, sir," the President replied.

That night, the President and I woke up on time at two thirty and we dressed quickly. I had prepared my clothes the night before, anticipating being groggy and grumpy. Being late would cost us a lick.

Off we went. Around the front of the cafeteria, heads bowed from fatigue, stepping in cadence with one another, we marched. We crossed under the arches, through the administration building, and out the front door. It was longer this way but it didn't matter. We needed time to wake up.

As we turned left on the sidewalk leading from the administration building to the chapel, we ran smack into Brother Greg. He was hooded, hands folded and hidden beneath his smock, his head pressed against his chest.

"Good morning, Brother Greg," I said, attempting to be polite.

He did not reply.

"They ain't supposed to talk when they got their hoods over their heads. Don't you know that?"

"No," I said, "I didn't know that."

"Well, now you do," the President said.

Brother Greg, like all of the Brothers, was a very holy man to me. His commitment to his God was inspirational and moving. Secretly, I envied him. To live life away from the marketplace, from the grinding pace of living, secluded, silent, and devout. Such was a desired way of life in my mind. Even Mother hinted one time that she suspected I would become a priest one day.

As Brother Greg drifted by me this morning, the President and I both saw teardrops in the corners of his eyes.

"I think he was crying," I said.

"You would be, too, if you had to get up every fucking morning at four o'clock. I'm going back." The President wanted no part of this.

"C'mon, Mitch . . . ain't much to it . . . let's go. Man, they'll kick your ass if you don't show up."

"Goddamn, I hate this. I know I'm not going to make breakfast tomorrow."

"I'll see if George will sign in for you," I said.

We entered the chapel just as Droo and Robo I were leaving.

"Fuck both of you," Droo muttered.

"Good morning," we both replied.

As we entered the sanctuary, our names were checked off and we stopped speaking to one another. The silence in the chapel was deafening.

As we headed down the main aisle, the ten-foot crucifix of Jesus hanging on the left side of the chapel was bearing down on me.

By the time I was in kneeling position at the front of the altar, I was feeling uneasy. Scared and immobile, I was unwilling to turn my head to see if He was watching me. I bowed my head, eyes wide and open, and repeated the Morning Watch prayer.

"Behold. You desire truth in the inward parts. And in the hidden part. You will make me to know wisdom. Purge me with hyssop, and I shall be clean. Wash me, and I shall be whiter than snow. Make me to hear joy and gladness, that the bones which You have broken may rejoice. Hide your face from my sins and blot out all my iniquities. Create in me a clean heart, O God. And renew a steadfast spirit within me. Know, then, if anyone is in Christ, he is a new Creation; old things have passed away. Behold, all things have become new."

I remained kneeling. I could feel my heart pounding, my skin pulsating, the rhythm of life like a moonlit river of silk flowing through me, around me, swirling and washing me, my heart and my will. Here, in the chapel, I was safe and sound.

The smell of the incense launched me back to the serene, Sunday hours spent throughout my childhood in my hometown church in Monroe.

There is a stain glass window in St. Paul's church that is dedicated to the memory of my grandfather, a man who died before I was ever born. There is listed the dates of his birth and death, his full name, and above that, a scene that depicts a woman coming to Jesus for healing in a vineyard. When I recalled that sight, there was a flood of emotional souvenirs and mnemonic reminders, relentless and powerful.

This early morning, this day of the Morning Watch, an

emotional flood permeated my mind. From the silence that enveloped the chapel, I remembered some of the words of the song found on page 243 of the hymnal in my hometown church.

> I sing a song of the Saints of God
> Faithful, loyal, and true.
> One was a fisherman
> And one was a priest
> And one was slain
> By a fierce wild beast
> And there's not any reason
> No, not the least,
> Why I couldn't be one, too.

I treasured my time there in front of the make-believe tomb and occasionally shifted my attention to the lingering winter wind swirling around the white oak branches outside.

Nothing moved in the chapel during that brief quarter of an hour. Not the air, the flowers, or the limbs of my body. When it was time to leave, the President and I barely spoke, for I sensed that he, too, encountered something worth being quiet about.

I was happy that we did not choose to speak and cherished the short, brisk walk back to our room.

But the Morning Watch is more than a religious theater where monks and would-be monks, priests, and devotees pay homage to the Christ. It is a playful time for the mice that roam the dark hallways late at night, unleashed from their cells, not to be stalked until morning time.

The reverent silence we shared all the way back to St. Patrick's quickly came to a halt when I opened our door.

"Goddamnit!" I yelled.

"Fucking-a!" the President yelled. "What in the hell . . ."

Laughter erupted all along the hall as we wiped from our eyes the smelly contents that fell from the bucket waiting for us when we opened our door. Water mixed with ketchup, mustard, salt, pepper, shaving cream, piss, toothpaste, dog shit, grass, dirt,

cologne, and a nucleus of unidentifiable foulness so rank that made
me want to vomit dripped slowly from our heads.

"Jesus!" the President said grinning. "I think it's time for a
war."

"Sonuvabitch! I'm gonna NNOKI somebody for this!" I said
in agreement.

"Shhh . . . Billy . . . Shhh! Somebody's down in the bathroom."
The President crouched, pointing in the direction of the noise
like an Irish setter.

"I know who did it. It's that bastard Yates!" I said surmising
the identity of the culprit.

"Bullshit, Yates is too lazy. C'mon," he said.

We changed clothes quickly, wiping the stinking muck and
sludge from our hair, the inside of our ears, and our chests and
backs.

We snaked our way to the bathroom and there they were.
Sammy and Watkins were hiding over in the corner, having a smoke,
choking on their laughter.

"Did you hear that damn can hit his head? We NNOKIed
their asses," Sammy said hysterically.

"I bet he's still stinking in the morning!" Watkins wheezed.

"Stupid a-hole! He didn't even look!" Sammy said, shaking his
head back and forth, not believing their caper had succeeded in
such a magnificent manner.

"Yeah, but the sound of that can on his fucking head!" Watkins
said.

They both joined in, mocking me, imitating the sound of the
can hitting my head. They were holding their noses in a futile
attempt to restrain the joy of their triumph.

The President and I tiptoed back down to the room.

"What do you want to do?" he asked.

"Let's get cleaned up real quick. And then, get that can of
right guard spray and get your lighter . . . the one you hide in
your literature book and c'mon . . . we've got work to do." I said.

We grabbed towels, washed up as best we could, and changed
clothes. With military-like stealth we soundlessly weaseled our

way down to the bathroom. They were still there. Their backs were against the half wall that separated the showers from the toilets, sitting on their fannies, their knees up to their chins, still laughing, enjoying their short-lived victory.

We positioned ourselves kneeling on the opposite side but facing them. The President held the can and began to slowly move his hand along the wall with my arm moving just underneath his, the lighter just beneath the tip of the canister.

When the President pinched me, I flipped the lip while he pushed the spray cylinder and the flame shot out at least two feet right at their heads. Sammy and Watkins screamed at the top of their lungs. In a New York minute, there was bedlam.

"This way!" the President yelled.

Panicking, looking only for an escape route, we tore down the stairs, out the back door, around the back of the cafeteria and into the chapel again. We sat in the back and waited for the changing of the guard. We walked out with the departing group.

Upon entering the dormitory for the second time that night, Mr. Winton grabbed us.

"The two of you were supposed to be back at three fifteen. Where have you been?"

"Mr. Winton, it was difficult to leave. It was real meaningful to me," the President said.

"I agree, sir. I got a lot out of it. I'd like to go back again," I said.

"What's that smell?" he asked.

"Dog poop," I replied. "Mitch stepped in dog poop."

So, good old Mr. Winton let us go back for another tour of duty at the chapel and I started over with my prayer and my feeble thanks for the gift that Christ had offered.

It was four fifteen before we got back to the room. Sammy and Watkins were still up and the President snuck down to their room to trade lies about the night and argue about whose trick had been the most ingenious.

I scribbled off a quick letter to Mother.

Dear Mom,

 Here's the poem that I wrote for Mr. Winton:

And now cometh the Spring.
The stirring songs she sings
will seize the nude forest
and the trees will stretch out their sonorous
and swaying branches to hear the piping song;
and there will be Life.

 Well, that's it. It's not worth anything but it's the best I can do. In case you don't know, it's a lyric-free verse. You always said you wanted to read the kind of stuff I was writing, so here it is.

 Man, the priests up here go crazy over Easter. Mitch and I had to get up at two thirty tonight to go stand watch in the chapel. It was really an OK experience. James Agee wrote about this, I think. He must have seen something in it that I don't. We have a service today that will last about three and a half hours. I dread it.

 B-Czar dressed up like Jesus but it was OK There was another priest here today. He's a pretty cool guy. His name is Father Fly. I got a chance to meet him.

Love,

Billy

CHAPTER 10

Mr. Gautier

As spring wove its magic and the hope of going home for vacation was shifting from fantasy to reality, my relationships with a couple of teachers blossomed.

Mr. Gautier was an introverted man and a thinker. He was my French instructor and was a loving and well-intentioned teacher. He treated me with respect, his expectations of me were firm, and his love for me was unshakable. He reeked of the smell of cigarettes when he spoke but he was customarily quiet and did not speak until his words gathered shape and weight.

It was very awkward at first, having had no daily experience of being with a loving man in my life. Manhood to me was characterized by such a distorted point of view that it would suffice to say that Mr. Gautier presented to me an antithesis of my past experiences and I initially wrote him off as being odd and queer. I felt uncomfortable around him in the beginning so I did not request his counsel nor engage him in leisure talk. He, however, sought me out.

What made it all the more difficult to avoid him was the fact that there were only four of us in the French III class. You were right there under his watchful eye for a full hour and there was no escaping. It was not that he was anything less than the good teacher he was. Being exposed to a level of love and concern that was consistently shown to me resulted in my hesitation. It caused me to be needlessly suspicious, for everything that I had learned in my life up to that time gave me reason to question his motives. I didn't know how to trust.

The French III class was a beginner's study of literature and I was soon addicted to serious reading. I was proud just to be carrying my textbook and would put it on top of the stack under my arm so that everyone could see what I was reading. I may not have understood calculus or physics, but I was one of four who had this one.

Mr. Gautier's voice was very soft. His understanding of literature was outstanding and I listened intently to his marvelous examinations of the works he selected for us. As time went by, he presented us with many different ways of thinking in the world, many different kinds of philosophies and many different choices of living in this world.

Perhaps it was because of my small town upbringing in North Carolina that caused me to feel so excited about this new path of learning. His intellectual prodding had found a safe haven in my mind and I was becoming more and more grateful to him.

His lessons were excavations into my crystallized way of thinking and when enough had been emptied out, he struck with awesome clarity. My moments of readiness were always acknowledged and he never ceased to take advantage. I was proud to be in his class.

"*Bonjour, Monsieur,*" I said.

"*Bonjour, Guillaume, comment allez-vous ce matin?*"

"*Bien, Monsieur, je vais très bien, merci,*" I said.

"*Comment va votre mère?*" he asked.

"*Bien, elle va très bien, Monsieur,*" I replied. "Mr. Gautier, is that your book?" I asked, pointing to the book lying on his desk.

"Yes. Would you like to borrow it?" he replied.

"Is it any good?" I asked.

"*Délicieux!*" he said.

"I promise," I said, "to bring it back when I'm done.

"I don't think it will take you a long time. The author is German, you know."

I thumbed through pages, estimating the time I would need.

"Thanks, I mean, *merci,* Monsieur," I said.

"If you like that one, there's another I would recommend. It is a book for which he received the Nobel Prize for literature."

"Well, thank you. I'll see if I like this one."

I strolled out of his office with his copy of *Siddhartha*. I wrote to Mother about it.

———————————

For the first time since I've been here, I'm getting caught up in my reading. It might interest you to know the books we've read in English this year.

Here they are: *1. Death in the Family 2. The Great Gatsby 3. The Scarlet Letter 4. The Crucible 5. Billy Budd 6. Adventures of Huckleberry Finn 7. The Red Badge of Courage.*

I couldn't stand reading the *Scarlet Letter*. That's the most boring book in the entire world. In theology, I read *Doing the Truth* and *The Gospels According to Peanuts*. In history, we've read *Tale of Two Cities*. In French, we read a lot of excerpts from great French works, and I really like the philosophical stuff. There's a German guy that I like reading on the side, but some of it's hard to understand. His name is Hesse. It's like I'm in his book. Mr. Gautier is pretty smart, Mom.

———————————

There was little doubt what was happening to me in the hour a day I spent with him was spilling over into my other classes. When the April eighteenth grades went out, Mr. Jordan, my English teacher, was quick to notice the positive changes.

———————————

Billy is cheery, optimistic in class, and his contributions are among the best.

———————————

Mother was pleased and I set making honor roll the last grading period as a goal. Sammy, on the other hand, had taken a dive in a couple of areas, most notably, geometry. On the back of his geometry report card, Father Dunston stated,

---

Sammy wastes almost all his class study time. He does not seem to care about his marks at all.

I understood Sammy's dilemma well. There was an ebb and flow to all life at St. A., and that included grades. But both of us knew well that we would survive whatever calamity came our way, and we took the slides in grades with a grain of salt. We were both in thick with several faculty members, and our friendships with other boys were secure and life-giving.

Shortly after our grades went home, Mr. Gautier invited Sammy and me over for supper, an event that became a monthly custom.

Mr. Gautier had two adopted children. They were clever children and were exceptionally well mannered. We gathered at the table to give thanks and when the blessing was over, began passing the plates of food.

"Pass the bread, please," Sammy said.

As the talk and dinner sounds continued, a whirlwind overcame me.

The thing I feared the most about suppertime was his mere presence. If I had had the nerve, I would have eaten in the backyard every night because of my fear of him. The sight of my stepfather coming home toward dusk, the beige pickup truck pulling in the driveway, was enough to send me racing into the woods. Suppertime was prime time for his wrath and hostility.

We ate supper on a table he had built himself. It was a very shiny, glossy smooth table made from pine. The top of the table rested on a solid, eight inch wide, waist-high, rectangular storage space for brooms and mops that spanned the length of the table.

Once seated, my parents could not see my legs or feet, nor could I see theirs.

Sammy and I had a system for sitting at the table that accomplished two things. Sitting on the far ends of the bench made it more difficult for him to slap you and the one who sat on the far right hand side against the wall was responsible for stuffing unwanted vegetables in a jug that we kept hidden under the bench. Sitting on that end might keep you out of his reach but you still had the problem of not getting caught removing the broccoli.

One evening, we were going through the ritual of commands.

"Sit up straight," he said.

"Get your elbows off the table," he said.

"Put your napkin in your lap," he said.

"Don't eat and drink at the same time," he said.

"Don't stir your tea too loud. Just wiggle the spoon, don't slam it around," he said.

"Don't bring your mouth to your glass, take the glass to your mouth," he said.

"Wipe your mouth."

The militarized repetition produced emotional paralysis. I wondered how he dared mutter grace, meals being a chance for him to unload his rage and venom on children who were capable of nothing but love even to the point of adoring the person they hated the most. In the beginning, I blamed God for having brought him into my life.

Given a choice, I would have preferred to starve. But as children, we serve ourselves up well to the unspoken laws of being responsible for the well-being of the parent, and serve as recipients for their shortcomings. With each blow, we cradle the projected persecution sanctioned by the world around us, minimizing, as best we can, the crushing hurt of each wound that rattles the marrow of our bones.

This night Mother made a fine supper, but Nolan was in one of his moods. After grace things were quiet. The rattling of silverware, plates shifting, ice cracking, napkins being unfolded, the bench sliding forward, the knife hitting the plastic tray after slicing through the stick of butter. We knew better than to initiate a conversation on our own.

"Pass the bread," I said in a low voice.

My stepfather leaned across the table and struck me so quickly that I had no idea what I had done. His hand landed across the right side of my face, and I reeled backwards.

"Pass the bread, please!" he yelled.

"Pass the bread, please," I said, beginning to cry.

He handed me the small breadbasket. As I was reaching in underneath the warm napkin to take a roll, he dropped the breadbasket on the table, grabbed my arm, pulled me forward, and slapped me across my face.

"Never take the food! Take the bowl it's served in and then serve yourself!" he screamed.

I remained at the table, crying.

"If you keep up, I'll give you something worth crying about. Now, shut up and eat your food!"

I remained helpless to confront this violent man, but I was sure it would pass in time. Like a small child, I believed that if I covered my eyes, the monster could not see me.

"Mrs. Gautier, this is delicious! Thank you very much for having us," I said.

"Oh, you're so welcome. Mr. Gautier is very proud of each of you. Having you for supper is a way of showing that to you," she replied.

I knew that Mr. Gautier was very proud of Sammy, but I knew that I was his favorite. He never came right out and said it, but I knew it and I think that Sammy knew it, too.

"How is everything going, Billy?" Mr. Gautier asked.

"It's fine. I'm pretty sure I already have a summer job, which is good."

"What job is that?" he asked.

"I'll be doing construction work. The work is hard, but I enjoy it. The only problem is there's not much free time at the end of the day. By the time I get home, take a shower, and get something to eat, it's time to go to bed. I'm usually too tired to do anything else."

"Sam, will you be working with Bill?"

"Yes, unfortunately," Sam said. "I don't like working outdoors and sweating like Billy. I want to get a job working at a pro shop at a golf course. I love golf."

The chitchat continued for another half hour after the meal, and we were soon off to study-out at 7:00. It was an uneventful evening spent fulfilling the usual rigorous expectations and academic objectives.

It being late spring, however, all the boys knew that the letters of invitation were going to be mailed within days to the boys that the school wanted back the following year. Casualties were drawing near.

As we prepared for lights-out, a group of us gathered in the hall, sitting, backs against the wall.

"I wonder if they'll invite me back," the President said. "I don't think they will," he concluded with regret.

"I promise you they will," I said. "Don't worry about it anymore, not for one second."

"Your problem," Frankie said, "is that you're a fuckhead. You're always late for classes and for some reason, no matter how many times Speedy calls your name out after lunch and paddles your Carolina ass, you just don't get it. Just show up on time. If you're not late to anymore classes," he continued, "I bet you'll be fine. Where would we be without our President?"

"Nope," Bark said, "the reason he's not going to be invited back is because he's from South Carolina, and those are the stupidest people on the planet."

"Oh," the President replied, "and people from Florida are smart?"

"Hey," Flat Tire added, "Miller's from Florida if that helps any. He's the smartest guy in the school."

"Well," the President replied, "if it helps you any, go fuck yourself."

Before long, we were laughing hard, snorting loudly, and putting chokeholds on one another for reminders of friendship.

I felt safe and assured in my invited return and soon stumbled to my bed where that night, I fell quickly asleep. This night, the nightmare returned.

I awoke terrorized and sweating. I lay breathless.

To the best of recollection, I had this dream for the first time when I was around twelve or thirteen years old. I remember clearly that when I awoke, my bladder was about to burst. As I surveyed the room, Sammy was sound asleep.

I needed to use the bathroom but the pain of a beating was still strong on my backside. I could take no chances of running into my stepfather in the hall or coming out of the bathroom. Waking him when I flushed the toilet was possible and would result in painful consequences.

Instead, I went to the closet and switched on the light. I stepped inside, closed the door and pissed as quietly as I could into an old boot. I returned to bed and remained awake until morning's light.

This night at St. Andrew's, I cautiously moved down the hall to the bathroom, unable to distinguish my true whereabouts. I think I urinated in the toilet. I came to a halt when I realized I did not know where I was.

As I stood frozen and breathless I knew I was not in my room. Oh God, I thought, I am alive in this dream. Please let me out, please, please, let me out.

Soon, time passed and without explanation, I was back in my room, holding on to the square iron frame of my bed. I climbed in and buried my head in the pillow. What happened to me? Someone, please tell me what is happening to me.

As a child's screams fade to silent sobbing and no comfort is forthcoming, relief is found in emptiness, a void, where only the child can escape. It is often done through imaginary worlds, people, and feelings. The child can begin to ascend the wounds by being above it all, achieving, succeeding, and living out a grandiosity that is shallow, pretentious, and meaningless. Or the child can become the wound itself and pull inward, becoming depressed and lifeless, seeing the wound everywhere around him, burdened and low to the ground. But wounded both will remain.

CHAPTER 11

The Coming of Christ

Baseball season was three months of timeless, uninterrupted ecstasy.

On the very first day of practice, as I was on the way to the gym, I was approached by Timmy Presley, an unimportant senior who posed no threat.

"Hey, Billy," he said, "I hear you're going out for baseball."

"Yep," I said.

"What position?"

"Pitcher and third," I mumbled.

"I can tell you right now there's no need to try out for third because I play third. It's my position."

I turned to see if there were other sixth formers around him.

"Is that supposed to mean something to me, asshole?" I asked, almost begging for a fight.

"You little dickhead, you better shut up," he said, when suddenly, George came into sight.

"Hey, George," I said. "What's going on?"

I turned and chose to wait for my guardian.

Timmy left me and went alone.

A half hour later, Coach Landers was starting infield.

"Let's go, boys. Go to the position you're trying out for. Let's hustle."

Minutes into our first practice, he was hitting some tough shots. An infield fly, one headed straight up into the clouds.

"I got it . . . I got it!" Presley yelled.

Timmy was waving everybody off, and he moved in for the catch.

We watched the ball sky upwards as though it was never coming down, while watching Presley shuffle in circles for the catch. It was obvious that trouble was descending.

When the ball came down, it never touched his glove but hit him smack in the eye, sending him to the ground screaming.

"Oh my God!" Yates screamed. "Did you see that?"

We ran to him and watched him squirming in pain, his hands covering his face.

"Jesus," Weaver said, "is that his eye sitting out on his face?"

"Oh, my God!" Yates yelled. "It knocked his eyeball out!"

We held no loyalty to this casualty and moved back for the coaches to administer first aid. We, the "Fifth Form," could have cared less. With one high-fly, Timmy was out for the rest of the season.

The two weeks of practice were sheer bliss. At the end of practice one day, we jogged to the gym, the lake to our left.

"There's a covey of quail in those bushes," Yates said, "I saw them go in there."

We slowed down and crept toward the underbrush.

"Shhh," Lankesford pointed.

We moved closer and closer till our faces were pinned against the brush. When the covey took to the air and startled everyone, we threw ourselves on the ground, laughing.

My stepfather raised quail, trained birddogs for people, and was an avid hunter. Of the many chores we had, feeding the quail he kept in cages in the backyard was my favorite.

Sometimes, when I went to feed them, they would all bolt up at the same time and it would scare me. Sometimes, some of them would get away before I had time to close the door.

I would go screaming into the house.

"They got out! They got out!"

And whoever was left in the house came storming out.

"Grab the fishing nets!" my stepfather yelled.

Off through the bushes we would head after those innocent birds. But I never caught one once they left the cage. I wanted them free. Free from this place, free from the dogs, free from the cages. If only I could have been one of them, I dreamed.

I was nearing the end of my first year at St. Andrew's and I was happier than I had ever been in my life. I had gained thirty pounds from three squares a day and had gained the respect of my teachers except for my advisor, Van Broughton, who didn't care for me.

As we were nearing final grades, I managed to recover from a dismal beginning to an illustrious end. I wasn't honor roll, but I was hanging tough.

As a result of my athletic efforts, I was being initiated into the Varsity Club, the most prestigious advancement I had made. But the pain of going through the passage of rites in order to belong to this tribe was much less welcomed.

Because George Walker was, thankfully, my initiator, I felt certain I would have to undergo less than what was extracted from other boys. The very first day dispelled that myth.

"All right, McNeal, get your ass down there on the cement right now!" He was grinning ear to ear.

"C'mon, George, don't do this to me. There's no need to do this," I pleaded.

"Shut up, lamebrain, and open your mouth!"

Two stories up, perched in the windows, the Varsity Club members were sitting, with Lizard hovering above me. And suddenly there was airplane music, the sounds of combat and machine-gun fire. I saw an outstretched hand directly above my head two stories up.

"Yep," I thought to myself, "that's an egg."

"Drop your bombs, gentlemen, drop your bombs!" someone yelled.

One by one, eight in all, they fell. One fell right on my face, others on my head, face, and chest. Only one missed.

"We have casualties!" I heard someone yell. "There's blood everywhere!"

Then came the blood poured from bottles of ketchup stolen from Granny's kitchen. When the ketchup ran out, their collective imagination invented a substitute.

I thought to myself that if becoming a man meant going through ordeals like this, I wanted no part of it. But being in this tribe was a big deal and pulled me up and away from the status quo. The few, the proud, the mustard-drenched.

I lay on the liquid-soaked concrete waiting for the next air raid.

When I was replaced with another body, George took me to the side.

"Billy, I have a surprise for you," he said, handing me a bullfrog.

"What am I supposed . . . you're not going to make me . . . c'mon George, don't . . ."

"Unzip 'em," he said.

I unzipped my trousers. He pulled my briefs out, placed the frog snugly in my crotch and instructed me to zip my pants back up.

"Wear the frog in your underwear for the rest of the day and he damn well better be alive at supper."

"He's moving . . . am I allowed to . . ."

"You're allowed to do anything you want as long as he stays in your britches. If I find out you took him out, you're in deep shit."

Throughout the morning, the Varsity Club members were quick to hand check the frog to make sure he was still there and I had no intention of taking him out.

The frog did a great deal of squirming around for a couple of hours but died sometime in the middle of Father Perkinson's European history class. With no or very little air, it was more than the frog could endure.

"Jesus, McNeal, what did you kill him for?"

"George, I didn't kill him. He died because he couldn't breathe. He keeled off sometime during Perkinson's class."

"How do you know?"

"Well, he started squirming a lot, then jerked a little, and then went limp. I mean limp. He died right there."

"Doesn't matter. You'll get another one tomorrow."

"C'mon George, don't do this to me again."

George accepted the frog's death and I was excused from this part of the ordeal.

But for seven more days and nights, we underwent hell to belong to this elite club. Torture of all kinds. Liquids of all descriptions. The worst was yet to come and everyone knew it. We just did not know when.

Lizard Baldwin despised Harry Beauchamps, a day student from Sewanee. Harry was a fine athlete but was still a day student. Lizard hated Harry and initiating him in the Varsity Club must have served someone's sadistic purposes.

There was a small crowd that began to gather at the quad.

"Put your arm around him," Lizard said.

Harry slid his arm around the tiny fourth former who sat frozen and breathless. The little fourth former just happened to be in the wrong place at the wrong time and Lizard had nabbed him coming around the dormitory.

"Tell him you love him and you want him to be your girlfriend," Lizard laughed.

Harry obeyed.

"Blow in his ear and kiss his neck," Lizard said.

"I'm not going to . . ."

"You're not going to what? I said blow in his fucking ear and kiss his neck, asswipe. Do it or else."

Harry complied, submitting to the humiliation.

"Hold his hand," Lizard decreed.

This continued for ten minutes, bringing Harry to tears.

"Shut up, Beauchamps, shut your trap," Lizard said.

Suddenly, Lizard's eyes grew excited.

"I know what the hell to do with you, Beauchamps. Keep your ass right here till I'm back. You better be holding Willard's hand when I get back."

Lizard returned intoxicated with his new idea.

"Stand up Beauchamps, arms out," Lizard said.

Before us, in a little less than fifteen minutes, Harry was transformed from Harry Beauchamps, Varsity Club initiatee, to Jesus on the way to the cross. Harry stripped, and Lizard wrapped a white sheet around himself, barefoot, and sleeveless. Another senior made a makeshift crown of thorns from small twigs from the St. Dominic's bushes, and Lizard wrapped a couple of unused, rotten two-by-fours together to make a cross.

"Now, you're going to take a little walk, lamebrain. Go down to the gym and stand on the edge of the track. There's a soccer match and everyone will get a good look at you."

"I don't think that's very good idea, Lizard," Dwight said.

"Nobody will find out. Are you ready, Beauchamps?"

"You're going to regret this," Harry replied submissively.

"You're going to regret it if you don't get your ass down there," Lizard commanded.

Harry protested vehemently but bodily harm was his only other choice. He took orders and the Christ marched off to his crucifixion.

We snaked along behind him, careful not to get too close. Being identified as part of this muddled conspiracy was deadly.

"This is going to be good," Frankie said.

"I'm glad it's not me," I said.

I never believed Lizard would force Harry to go all the way with this joke because, even though he was a prefect, the risks for Lizard were too severe. There are points in time when everyone goes too far and there is no pulling back. That day had come for Lizard Baldwin.

Harry trudged down to the track, imitating Jesus. All in all, he did a respectable job.

"You know, he's doing such a good job," Flat Tire said, "he ought to play Jesus in the Stations of the Cross next year. I mean, really, he's good."

As Harry approached the track, we hid behind the old school building to watch the show. Motionless, head bowed, he stood in his crown of pine twigs, facing the fans, creating a graphic, indelible moment for several hundred people.

As we watched, we noticed the game slowing and we heard a whistle blow. The referee stopped the game, and everyone turned to stare at Harry. The eyes of the entire soccer arena, its coaches and players, and its fans, were all fixed on Harry Beauchamps, the would-be Jesus, shoeless, on the cross.

"The shit's getting ready to hit the fan, boys. Make sure your Converses are tied 'cause our ass is grass if we stick around here," the President said.

"They'll kill him," I said, "Beauchamps is so stupid."

"It ain't Beauchamps they're going to kill," Latch said, "it's Baldwin."

From the stillness of the Christian landscape, like a dark-gray calm before a thundering storm, there was movement from the middle of the bleachers and we saw the top of the old man's head rising slowly. It was the Czar.

While Harry remained to further serve this inevitable tragedy, we tore out of there as if our lives depended on it. There would be hell to pay for this.

"Fucking-a, man! They'll kick his ass for this!" Watkins screamed.

"The dorm! Head to my room!" Sam directed.

"I'm getting the hell out of here. Hide in the school building, school building!" Maguire pointed.

We waited anxiously through the evening knowing the ax was being swung. We received the news at the morning assembly.

Father Henry stood at the front of the hushed crowd and we knew he was angry.

"As you well know, gentlemen, I am very upset about yesterday's events and I expect anyone who had anything to do with this lame stunt to come forward now, this instant."

No one moved. No one dared twitch a muscle.

"In that case, I am going to assume that Mr. Bladwin was the only one involved besides Mr. Beauchamps, who is not with us this morning but to whom I have spoken."

Thanksgiving that none of us were involved filled this space.

"Mr. Baldwin has been stripped of his prefectship, is hereby placed on weekend bounds for the rest of the year, is being sent to supervised study, and is being removed from the Varsity Club. It is our hope that this kind of prank will not happen again."

"No, I don't think it will," I thought to myself.

"Oh, my God," Limpy whispered, "they kicked him out of the Varsity Club."

"Lizard's going to kill Harry," Droo muttered.

The assembly came to an end with none of us wanting to

make contact with any senior. They were on the prowl and would use this incident to vent their anger at what had happened to one of theirs.

But Father Henry's reality was not necessarily ours. To understand this event, an outsider must understand the hierarchy of the pack. Despite Lizard's decapitation, he retained his position among the student body, for there is an invisible order and rank to which all animals adhere. We were no different. Lizard went about his life as though nothing happened, and we stayed out of his way. Lizard was still the ruler of this kingdom, prefect or not.

As for Harry, he was harshly scolded for taking part and was sent back to the fold. Harry dared not mention how wonderful the taste of revenge was. Had one word slipped from his tongue, Lizard would have beheaded him. Surviving the ordeal was prize enough. Beauchamps, the Christ Jesus, was resurrected the following day and returned to class unscathed.

As the end of the year approached, bringing with it a lightheartedness of spirit and release of tension, I realized I had made a lot of progress in the classroom. Looking at myself academically was like walking through a fog. I didn't even know I was soaking wet until I decided to change my clothes. My progress was slow and unnoticeable on a daily basis but nonetheless, was present. Oddly, I felt smarter.

Mr. Jordan was the most complimentary and said,

Billy had a fine year here. He is outstanding in every facet of our life. In the classroom, his knowledge, his enthusiasm, his sincerity, all contribute to making the learning process an enjoyable experience for us all.

Mother attended the end-of-year ceremonies that were held in late May when all of the wild dogwood trees and azaleas were

still blooming. I was waiting for her where the highway meets the
school road.

As I sat rocking back and forth on the rock wall lining the
paved entrance, I glanced back over my left shoulder to ponder my
past year.

The campus was never more beautiful than this moment with
its annual carpet of pink and white that sprung up at every corner.
Manicured lawns, trimmed bushes, and the fresh scent of pine
and pollen permeated the view. I was more than content. I had
become a part of this school.

The three of us attended the awards ceremonies that took place
a day before graduation. It is a testy, tense, moment for all the
soon-to-be-seniors because the prefects for the upcoming year are
named on this occasion. It is the last announcement that is made
on the program.

The St. A. prefect is a god at school, in charge of a dormitory,
and of other students. Decisions of life and death weigh in the
balance as the prefect inspects each room for cleanliness and proper
order. He is automatically on the Student Council, compels respect
and space, and is entitled to numerous privileges not shared with
any other classmates, not even other seniors. A prefectship was the
treasure desired by all.

Father Henry and Father Benjamin, the Prior, were seated
with the senior class on the stage in the newly built school
building. It was a glorious moment for all faculty, students
and parents. The building was being dedicated to Father Harvey
Sherwin who had faithfully served St. Andrew's School for many
years and whose son, Allen, was to be a math teacher at St.
Andrew's the next year.

Mr. Sherwin was born in Troy, New York, in 1902 and at an
early age became a missionary at the Liberian Mission of the Order
of the Holy Cross. He had done various things in his life, which
included service as a school principal, rector, and arch-deacon. He
completed his time with the Holy Cross in Africa by aiding the
escape of German refugees during World War II and had been the
business manager, bursar, and chaplain of St. Andrew's from 1948

to the time of his death in early 1964. He was described as a dedicated priest, a wise counselor, and a loyal friend to Father Henry.

A huge crowd gathered in the new school as a stunning and elegant painting of Father Sherwin was mounted and blessed, a small crucifix hanging above it.

"If every boy at St. Andrew's were to model himself after Father Sherwin, his life would be rich, rewarding, and a blessing to others," Father Benjamin said.

As the dedication ceremony came to a close, faces lit up like fireflies if for no other reason than the fact that we were going home in two days for the summer.

Father Henry began with the academic awards, the scholarships and the names of the colleges to be attended by the graduates. But the golden apples were the athletic awards and the announcement of the prefects. Every bit of chatter, every muffled word, every slur out of the corner of the mouth was about the prefects.

"I'll bet you that Weaver's head prefect," Sammy said to me.

"Five big ones say that Flat Tire gets one," the President said jabbing his finger in my side.

"Fuller's my man," I said. "I know he's going to get one."

"Bullshit, Maguire's an ass kisser," Frankie said, "he'll get one. You watch and see."

They were at the end of the athletic list when baseball came up. I knew who was going to get the prize.

Coach Winton took the podium.

"Most valuable player for the 1968 season, a player who struck out only three times, maintained a batting average of .443, scored more runs than anyone else, and one of the meanest catchers I have ever coached . . . Sammy McNeal . . . McNeal II."

I was envious but happy for him. We stood up with a resounding round of applause. Mother was glowing. Even the seniors stood and that was quite a tribute. As he walked by me, I took his head with both hands, held his glance in mine, and said, "Nice going . . . you deserved it."

"Thanks," he said, "thanks."

As he returned with his prize in his hands, he tried not to smile but he was ecstatic. He was so happy he looked like he was going to cry.

The moment finally came to announce the prefects' names and the dormitories of which they would take charge.

There was a still hush and in the bosom of every mother and father present, the same wish was had: "My son, the prefect."

Father Henry took advantage of the caged emotion and delivered a stirring invitation to each boy to become his best. He was masterful at this because he meant it, and he said it with experience and authority. The seriousness soon trailed away, and everyone waited anxiously.

"I will now name the prefects for the 1968-1969 school year."

He paused, pretending to shuffle some papers.

"Dennis Weaver, head prefect, St. George's dormitory."

We leaped to our feet clapping and hollering. He deserved this honor a thousand times over.

"Ricky Duval, assistant head prefect, St. Henry's dormitory."

"What? Ricky? You've got to be kidding! He doesn't know the difference between his head and his ass! Good God," Duck whispered.

"Sammy McNeal, McNeal II, prefect St. Dominic's dormitory."

I thought Mother was going to die on the spot. And then I thought I would.

"Sonuvabitch, I swear, I've got put up with his stuff all summer. Jesus Christ, I don't believe it," I muttered to Duck.

"Jason Fuller, prefect, St. Patrick's dormitory."

"Fuller, Fuller, Fuller," the chant strengthened.

"Will Carver, prefect, St. Albans' dormitory."

"Bullet! Yes, sir! Copies homework faster than a speeding bullet!" the President said to anyone who would listen.

"Daniel Adamsworth, prefect, St. George's dormitory."

"Limpy! Go get 'em, Limp! Yeah, he deserved it . . . he . . ." Jody said.

"Like hell he did," the President snarled back, "the only reason he got it is 'cause he's been here five years. It's like time served or something like that."

"Peter Merchant, prefect, St. David's dormitory."

"Merch got lucky," I thought to myself.

"Billy McNeal, McNeal I, prefect, St. Joseph's dormitory."

Astonished, I looked at my mother. My mother turned to hug me as warmly as she had my brother, and I could see in her eyes that she was about to die from the sheer enormity of the situation. She was paralyzed with joy.

The ceremony came to an end and the audience was dismissed as Sammy and I remained breathless.

"Nice going, Billy," the President said smiling.

"Thanks . . . thanks," I said. "But I didn't deserve this."

Mother stopped to give an envelope she pulled from her purse to Brother James. I was being swept along with friends out of the building. We were bouncing every step on our way home for the summer.

I cradled a shiny new apple in my pocket as I joined in with the other new seniors singing quietly our national anthem.

"We're the boys from old St. A. and we don't give a damn.

"We go to school, and break the rules

"And flunk the damn exams.

"So to hell with the east, to hell with the west,

"To hell with the whole damn crew,

"If you don't go to old St. A., to hell, to hell with you."

We didn't even make it past the exit of the new building before Father Henry caught up with me.

"Billy, I expect a great deal from you next year. You kept your agreement with me this year. I am certain you will respond in the same manner next year."

"Yes, sir," I said, "I will."

CHAPTER 12

Smashing Johnny Hannah

As the summer drew quickly to a close, Sammy and I struggled to complete our summer reading in preparation for the United States history class that Mr. Van Broughton taught. I dreaded it.

Everyone was required to read *Uncle Tom's Cabin*, *The Making of the President 1960*, *The Strange Career of Jim Crow*, and *The Age of Jackson*. He tried to frighten us in his letter by warning us of the "simple but extensive" tests we would take upon arriving back at school. His instructions about Theodore Black's book were over my head.

It might be exceedingly helpful in understanding the machinations through which the candidates will go in the near future. Pay special attention to methods as described by Mr. Black. Also, you might take particular notice of the candidates and compare them to those in this upcoming election.

It was as Sammy said. "He thinks we're in college or something."

Mr. Van Broughton was kind enough to include his address at the Carolina Yacht Club at Wrightsville Beach, welcoming our correspondence. I am certain it was a tough, hot summer for him.

Updates from Father Henry were arriving on a frequent basis

and refreshing our memories of reading obligations and upcoming changes in our lives at St. Andrew's. He wrote a letter on July 11, 1968 to the parents of all the old boys.

———————

The cloudy skies and rainy climate of this morning at St. Andrew's as I begin to prepare this letter to you are a welcome relief from what has been so far an extremely warm and dry summer on the mountain. We are relaxing in the relief of a rather long and gentle rain that is soaking into the ground and reviving our grass and trees and all growing things. The campus, as usual at this time of year, gives an appearance of outside calm and quiet, dictated by the fact that 160 rather noisy boys are not with us.

Some members of the faculty are away for the summer, engaged in various projects. Mr. Jordan is studying in the graduate school at Vanderbilt in the field of English under a grant from the National Foundation. Colonel Shuford has been ordained a deacon and will be studying shortly at Middle Tennessee State University in the area of guidance, and Mrs. Shuford will be at Auburn soon in the graduate school of English. Mr. Winton is at Auburn for the entire summer, studying in the graduate school of English. Mrs. Sherwin attended a reading institute at Berea College in Kentucky earlier this summer. We expect her son, Andy, who will be joining the faculty this year, to arrive from his Peace Corps service in Nigeria some time this month. Father Hazelton has just returned from a conference for school chaplains at Princeton University and is beginning his studies for the summer at the Graduate School of Theology at the University of the South. Mrs. Chamberlain will soon be leaving for an important CAP conference, and Father Chamberlain is busy this summer preparing a scholarly paper for presentation at the fall meeting of the Tennessee Philosophical Association. Mr. Van Broughton is once more instructing in his specialty, sailing, at the Yacht Club at Wrightsville Beach, North Carolina, and Mr. Lucas is in New Mexico. Mr. Spangler is once more busy at the Assembly at Monteagle where he is recreational director, and Mr. Stevenson, Mr. Gautier, and Father Dunston are all busy at the school.

He was dutiful as always in spelling out his expectations with the summer reading list and suggested that many of us consider buying new school blazers which were free from stains and frayed edges which would not be tolerated. He ended his letter with a predictable note:

I hope that you and your boy are having a refreshing, restful, and profitable summer. Help your boy to maintain the regularity and simplicity of life that he has been leading at St. Andrew's. All of us here join in sending our very best wishes.

This summer was less simplistic than it was a frenzied, calculated panic. Every penny we earned and every weekend we spent was woven into the fabric of this thing called going off to school. It was a ritual of departing to more productive, seasonal grounds where all the tribes' goods were loaded and tied down, each individual having a specific chore to carry out. It seemed to go on all summer long, until Sam and I were told to be sure and drop by certain relatives' houses for one last gathering. That was a sure sign that a final goodbye was lurking patiently and the 64th academic year at St. Andrew's was soon to be underway.

While I pushed myself to prepare for early football and was anxious to rejoin the boys I had not seen in three months, I was even more excited about joining the student body as one of Father Henry's selected prefects.

One of eight chosen to serve, I wanted to live up to his expectations of me and for a while, this sense of grandiosity was useful in protecting me, allowing me to climb above the worries and confusion that so often overtook me.

For who I was in the summer of 1968 was not the same boy who had left home in August 1967. I could not accurately detect the changes although I felt them in my body. I could not describe them although I heard them speak in my mind. I could not convince anyone of them because a dangerous self-doubt still lurked nearby.

I wanted to convince myself I was one of Father Henry's hand-picked but it seemed there was another who spoke, mostly negatively, and warned of impending doom. I did not know which one I was.

As the summer months waned and grew hotter, late afternoon and weekend trips to the public pool were standard. There was one occasion that sparked a force inside of me I never knew existed.

"Do you know that guy?" Sammy asked.

The public swimming pool was half deserted. I rolled over on my stomach, allowed my head to lean slightly over the edge of the sundeck, watching the coming and going of all the mischievous, little children, palms loaded with penny candy. Suddenly, to the left, I saw him. He was climbing the ladder to the high dive area pushing a little kid half his size out of the way, and thumping him on the ear.

"Get out of the way, you little dipshit," the bully said.

"Who do you think . . ."

"Better shut up or I'll knock the shit out of you."

Up the ladder he went uncontested.

Johnny Hannah picked on me from the time I entered the fourth grade to the time I went to high school. He was a skinny, thin-legged kid who enjoyed the protection of some of his older buddies who amounted to nothing more than he did. But they were bigger.

"Yeah, I know him," I said. "That's Johnny Hannah. Don't you recognize him?" I asked.

"I remember him," Sammy said.

"Yeah, I remember he would always push me off the bus at East Elementary School and start slapping me around for five to ten minutes in front of everybody. He used to beg me to hit him back but I knew better 'cause if I did, he'd kill me."

"He's an asshole," Sammy said.

"Yep, he is. But I wonder what he has to say about that today."

I stood up and headed toward the diving area.

"Billy, don't go down there, come back," Sammy said.

Seeing Johnny created an instantaneous response in my body. I stiffened and tightened every muscle, completely unaware of what was happening to me. I walked to the metallic ladder and waited murderously close, hoping he would step up to dive again. I doubted he would recognize me. It would not matter.

As he broke in line again and pulled the kid's hair that stood in front of him, I was filled with rage, rendering me virtually unaware of what I was doing. I dove recklessly into this scene from which there was no backing out.

As his hands reached to grab hold of the ladder, and his right foot headed for the first rung, I grabbed his right shoulder and pulled him down. As he turned, I drew back and buried my fist in his face, his head bouncing off of the fifth ladder step, careening forward back to my hands, his face now covered with his own blood.

The warm red dripped steadily from beneath his left palm. I grabbed his head by his hair and drug him over to the brick wall, threatening him every inch of the way.

"If you ever touch anybody again here at the pool, if you ever say one word to anybody, I'll kill you! Don't dare raise your hand at me, don't talk at me, don't ever cross in front of me 'cause if you do, I'll kill you, you sorry good-for-nothing sonuvabitch! Do you understand me? Look at me when I'm talking to you! You remember me? Look at me, Hannah! Goddamnit, I'll kill you if you ever touch anybody out here again! I promise you, I'll kill you, you sorry piece of shit."

I threw him down on the concrete where he lay crying. I stood over him, shaking. I was out of control.

I picked him up once more, and threw him against the wall where he remained, gathering his senses and trying to understand what in God's name had just happened to him.

As I turned to walk away, a crowd gathered to watch Johnny Hannah swallow what had been due him for a long time. I relished the encounter and felt I struck out at an opponent who had kept me at bay for what seemed to be a lifetime.

"What the hell is wrong with you, Billy?" Sammy yelled.

"Shut up," I said, "and leave me alone."

My explosive assault upon Johnny Hannah left me in a daze, for I realized I had acted the same way he once did. I was perplexed and oddly saddened. In spite of my attack, I justified every drop of blood that now lay mixed with the pool water on the concrete pad.

"He had it coming for a long time," I said to Sammy.

"You hurt him," Sammy said.

"So what? He deserved it," I explained.

"He will never bother me again. He will never touch me again," I thought to myself as I made my way past the concession stand and out the back door.

On August 15, nine days before my departure for school, Father Henry wrote a letter to all of the prefects, poignantly spelling out his feelings with regards to our selection as prefects. Whether I idealized and imagined the letter to be more than it was, it mattered not. It was my interpretation of this new endeavor and responsibility that catapulted me to a higher order of thinking and relating to the world.

I want you here in time to get settled down before any of the football players arrive on Sunday. We will plan to go out somewhere to eat a nice steak dinner on Saturday night, and we will then come back to the office for some discussion and conversation that night. I will let you know the rest of the schedule after you get here on Saturday.

There is one thing I particularly want to impress upon you now as you begin your final thinking about your duties. I believe that the most important and necessary attribute of a good prefect is that of integrity. I must be able to put full trust and confidence in the character and actions of each and every prefect. This is one thing that I will expect of you in the highest degree. I must know that I can trust you and that you will be honest with me and in your dealings with your boys and your dormitory master and other members of the faculty. This is a most essential quality. You must set a good example for your boys, obeying the rules yourselves. We must have absolute confidence and trust in each other, and I want to be sure that you know that I have to depend on you and put my full confidence in you and that I expect you to merit this.

Please give this your fullest thought before you come back to school, and come back determined to stand strong for honesty and integrity within your own lives and within the life of the entire student body.

I was motivated by his instructions and momentarily, no longer felt besieged by the littleness that seemed so prevalent in my life. This one opportunity afforded me the momentum and spark to be lifted above the crowd, to be admired. Father Henry began to whittle, mold, carve and shape the still green wood. My experience at this time in my life assured me that few older men conducted themselves with younger men quite that way, very naturally, and from mission and purpose. Father Henry was one of my first experiences of being around men as such. Men such as he are gifts to the younger ones.

But there is not enough consciousness in the boy to freely give himself over to such a mentor and it can be a haphazard game, one in which many young boys are missed. Besides, a healthy amount of resistance and questioning is needed on the part of the novice to avoid the pitfalls of lame acceptance of a yet unknown and untested mode of being.

For all of the boys at St. Andrew's, we had only inklings of the consequences of his influence on us. It would be years before the young boy stepped to one side in life, looked into the past, and saw the stepping-stones that had been deliberately laid before each of us.

August came abruptly and before anyone knew it, we were gone again. Sammy and I, cocky and secure, made our pilgrimage back to the mountain. It would be the last year we would share home together.

Who are our real families, our kin, the ones we call brothers and sisters and cousins who are so quickly removed and replaced by new friends, new lovers and long-distant comrades? Is it just by blood, by name that we are joined in family?

I saw a world that stretched beyond my most imagined possibilities and whose boundaries were being extended further and further every second of every minute. I wanted to know it, breathe it, cling to it, own it, and harness it. I wanted to know this vital exploration of the nucleus of life, this journey of spirit. I wanted to be swallowed up by it, to know in the marrow of my bones, this new world built on seductive dreams of promise and ascension to the summit of a peak upon which I knew I could and would discover the Grail in all its beauty. My path would not be the one of my brother, the dutiful one.

Each of us had other families waiting on us, itching with expectations and renewed bonds. I missed my brothers at St. Andrew's and the men who taught there. Had I any idea of their worth and value in my life, I would never have even come back to North Carolina for the summer in the first place. In a strange way, the tables were now turned and I felt that in returning to St. Andrew's School, I was going back home.

The prefects, the gods of St. A., gathered apart from the rest of the kingdom to be adored and smothered with attention and well-wishes by the faculty and the Czar himself. It was a celebratory time for them and us. I felt admired by Father Henry, rewarded by the older men, and strategically moved forward by balancing arms and firm hearts.

Even if the entire scenario could be cynically portrayed as pretentious and weak in substance, a result of my imagination, it had its value. It was a passage, a permeation of ritual and pomp, through which no boy could walk unaffected. The message could be seen clearly in our glowing yet, frightened eyes even if we were unable to articulate exactly what the message was. Deep inside, we all knew what this was about. Become what you are capable of being.

The eight of us gathered to be knighted and to receive our scrolled instructions for governing and preserving our separate serfdoms, the laws of the land laid before us with uncompromising demand for loyalty and adherence to those laws. And the steak wasn't bad either.

Getting a free meal away from campus was one of the simplest but most enjoyable pleasures of all. Occasionally, a relative would pass through and take a boy out to eat at the Sewanee Inn or the Holiday Inn in Monteagle. It was such a relief to be removed from the daily grind of unrelenting discipline and constant expectation that it was, to a St. A. boy, what a vacation in Bermuda was to a man who worked fifty-one weeks of the year. To have a faculty member afford you the experience was all the more momentous.

In this case, it wasn't a faculty member but the Czar himself. No one had to be told a single word. The understanding of our selection was deep, and our paths were well marked before us like fluorescent road signs on the way to an unknown destination.

When we returned that night, I slept for the first night in St. Joseph's dormitory not as a student but as a prefect and I felt that difference in my veins.

I wrote two letters home that night before finally joining the others for some late night TV in the senior lounge in the basement. It would be our last night of careless and lazy meandering before early football began the next day and the game would be underway. We joked and hypothesized and cussed our way into the hour of two before knocking off for the night.

"I'll tell you one thing, if that stupid Brisbin fucks up one time, that bastard will be cleaning my room all year long," Limpy said.

"Yeah, right, Limpy. You love him and you know it," Fuller called back.

"Fuck you, Fuller," Limpy said, flipping Fuller off. "You're going to be cleaning up Palmer's mattress from where he beats off every morning."

Limpy was visibly angry and perturbed by Fuller's comments.

"Did you hear about that last year?" Sam asked.

"What, about Palmer?" Bullet perked up.

"I heard about it," I said.

"Yeah," Sammy continued, "he had a hole in his mattress at dick-level so he could jack off every morning."

"Man, that's gross," Weaver joined in.

"Just keep that leper away from my bed, end up with my dick catching a disease or something," Limpy said.

"Palmer said you didn't have a dick," Merch said.

Although he fought it, Limpy couldn't help but laugh.

As always, the conversation eventually turned to classes and inward but unannounced fears of massive homework and term papers. Most of us had been selected to be in the advanced English class taught by the Czar himself. The class was Early British literature.

We knew that nothing less than total preparation and prompt assignment completion would be acceptable or we would find ourselves removed. While I was thrilled at the prospects of being with Father Henry for an hour a day, I was apprehensive about his class because of the horror stories I had heard.

All of us were to have carefully selected roommates and were given a serious and mindful speech as how we should make that choice. I asked Steven Larue, the boy who had escorted me on my first tour of St. Andrew's, to share the duties. Duck was to arrive the next day and I went to bed that night impatiently waiting for the sight of him.

I slept late, skipping breakfast, and was awakened by his voice.

"You better get your ass out of bed, you lazy a-hole."

"Hey, man! When did you get here?" I said, twisting upward and out of bed. We hugged.

"About five minutes ago. I saw Sammy up the quad." He began sliding his suitcases in his closet. "They're all up there."

"Any new shit yet?"

"Yeah, two brothers, the Lawsons. One of them looks pretty stout."

"Don't know them. I haven't seen anybody yet," I said, yawning.

"Well, c'mon, let's get rolling. Let's go get Mrs. Taylor to open up. Dad just left and I forgot to take out a box of home-made cookies and shit that I left in the trunk, and I'm hungry," he said, looking around the room to see if I had any food lying around.

I dressed quickly and we rambled off to the school store to find Mrs. Taylor. With snacks in hand, we joined the others at the quad to watch the remainder of the new football boys arrive.

As suppertime neared and all of the football boys reported for roll call, each of us who arrived a day early as prefects found our way to the front of the line, seniors, and privileged at last.

I remembered George and Lizard and the others who scared me so badly on my first day. I quickly spotted two boys, the littlest of the whole gang who reminded me of myself, timid and visibly out of place.

On the other hand, they seemed to be having the most fun. They were like a couple of squirrels, into everything, intimidated by nothing, and always making some kind of noise. I found their presence inviting and was polite to each of them even though I did not speak.

They discovered quickly that finding a friend and someone to lean on was a prerequisite to surviving. They had only been here for several hours at best. They would do well.

It was a quiet evening spent partly alone at the lake and partly on the bench, shoulder to shoulder with Frankie and Hatch at the quad where Harry Beauchamps had evolved into the Christ.

Hopes were high for a good season and our desire to fulfill those hopes had been fed well. It was all we could talk about. We were ready to play. It was the only reason some of the boys came back.

This glorious year would change my life forever.

CHAPTER 13

Burr Rabbit in the Briar Patch

"Boys, listen up," Stevenson demanded. "We begin our first practice in thirty minutes. In less than twenty-four hours, some of you won't be here. You'll be on the phone with your mother wanting to go home. And why? Because you won't think you can make it another two minutes. And I can't stop you from calling your mother. But I can tell you this. We have a good group this year. We have a large number of returning seniors and we have a damn good chance of beating the Academy this year. I want to urge you to stick it out. It's not going to be easy but then again, if it were easy, there'd be a lot more of you here today. But there's not. The rest of them are at home, sleeping late, watching cartoons, eating their mommy's pancakes. You're here on the verge of getting your fannies trained into shape, to function as a team, not as individuals. That makes you different because you have the courage to be here and I promise you, if you make it through these ten days, you will be on the team. And I promise you if you make it through and don't quit, you will be a better person for it. I expect your best even when your body doesn't want to work anymore, when your mind wants to quit, when your heart wants to cry. Discipline, gentlemen, is our path and it is a path that once you decide to walk it, will provide you with the rewards you desire. We are winners and we will train like winners, act like winners, and play like winners. I'll see you in thirty minutes on the field, half pads. Weaver, you and Billy will lead the drills. Pick it up, gentlemen, pick it up," he finished, as we stampeded to the locker room.

The first day of practice was unusually harsh and viewed in its entirety by the new Prior, Father Lee Deter, who was dressed in a stark, white robe that flowed along the top of the wet blanket of green, the hem gathering patches of dead blades of grass as he walked.

"He served seven years of service in a leprosy colony in Africa," Duck said.

"How come you know all this shit?" Limpy asked.

"I read it in a bulletin. My mom showed me," Duck replied.

Father Deter was a distracting figure for me because I never saw anyone who looked so much like Jesus Christ in all of my life. He had such an engaging, focused look on his face that I first guessed that he was part of the coaching staff. While he did not speak, he would slap us on the back reassuringly and smile as we huffed past him. He knew we were hurting and his presence was a way of encouraging us, convincing us not to quit. He was there at every practice, even if just for a short time.

As expected, it took little time at all for our rowdiness to come to a halt as free time was safeguarded as a chance for a nap or just an hour or two of physical recovery. My illusions of thinking that I had come back in shape were quickly annihilated and I watched as the injuries mounted.

The second day, after thirty minutes of endless barking and hollering from the coaching staff, we went into grass drills and fumble-recovery. Two by two, we lined up and waited our turns, struggling to catch our breath, only to hear the whistle blow faster each time. Sammy was lined up beside the President when their turn came.

When the whistle blew and the ball was tossed ten yards away from them, they both tore after the ball, huffing and pounding breath, dirt and small clips of grass flying up from under their cleats. Sammy was faster than the President and moved low to the ground in position to cover the ball. As he did, he clutched the ball to his stomach, elbows high and extended.

As he began to roll to his right side, the President lowered his helmet and pinned Sammy's right side to the ground. There was a horrible sound as the ball rolled out from under the two of them.

"Oh God!" Sammy screamed, "Oh God!"

"Oh, my God, help!" the President said yelling.

Standing up with his right arm extended, his arm from the elbow to his hand flopping around like a cloth doll. Sammy's elbow had snapped.

I rushed to him but there was little I could do.

"It's all right, it's OK!" I said. "Just be still . . . just be still!" I yelled.

"Lay him down! Lay him down!" Stevenson commanded.

He was placed on the ground, his arm eventually secured on a moldy, one-by-one piece of wood with strips of Stevenson's T-shirt.

Shortly, an ambulance came careening around the dirt curve to the gym and took him away.

"Gentlemen, let's get back to work. There's nothing we can do now," Stevenson said.

We went immediately back to full speed even though I was no longer mentally there. My brother was hurt.

Sammy was operated on that night, pins being placed in his elbow and a cast from shoulder to hand. Mother was there at the hospital by early evening but I did not see her as she left the following morning after his operation, feeling certain that there was nothing more she could do.

Several days later Sammy was on the sideline, pacing up and down displaying the wound like a trophy. Like an aged boxer, he had fought a good fight but lost. Though he was gone for the season, the whole ordeal of early football remained for me a mission.

To console Sammy's plight, a letter arrived from Mother several days later. She was angry.

Dear Sammy and Billy,

I am waiting patiently for an explanation as to what happened Saturday before you left for St. Andrew's and assume it will be a good one. Otherwise, you can become accustomed to riding buses.

Billy, I found today that in addition to your other
debts, you also now owe me for your rather expensive steaks.
Since you did not ask my permission to do this, you might
be interested in knowing that you can no longer charge
anything to me anywhere. It was only necessary for you to
have asked.

The following day, Limpy bit the dust and Larson, a day student
from Cowan, ran into Flat Tire's leg, resulting in his arm being
broken in four places. Brothers of the knife, the early tragedies
now walked together.

It was like a club. If it did nothing more for Sammy, he earned
the nickname, Big Sam, which he would be called henceforth even
by his peers. He wrote Mother a letter when get-well cards started
streaming in.

I got everybody's letters yesterday. Although I was out of the
hospital, I still got the greatest feeling just thinking that everybody
cared enough to write. Those letters did more for me than you'll
ever know. Maybe I'm starting to appreciate the small things in
life.

Some kid was going to go over the hill and I knew about it. So
at the table (he sat at mine) I talked about toughing it out and
taking it like a man. After the meal, he walked up to me and told
me he decided not to run away. He said I got through to him. He
said I was the reason he had decided to stay.

He was right. He commanded respect about himself in spite
of his injury and absence from the game and he was listened to by
all of us. Mother wrote him back and tried to console him.

I know you are disappointed about not being able to play any more football, but you seem to have taken it very well. I know it isn't easy for you, but then, there are worse things . . . I suppose. But don't ask me what. I hope you're going to work hard and do well in your classes as it is a very important year as far as college is concerned.

As the hours passed spent between practice and sleep, deeper and more penetrating bonds were being built among us, the old boys, the seniors. I had my favorites but found that being with just about any one of them was enough, whether we were studying together or just listening to a new record album that came in the mail.

Duck and I were to be predominantly busy with directing and commanding a dormitory of mostly new boys consisting of sophomores and some juniors. Their first day on campus was repeated much as our arrival had been a year before, except this year I had little time for myself, helping with parents, and unloading suitcases.

Some looked frightened and discouraged. I watched one boy dragged by his father to his ground floor room. Others accepted the unfolding event with grace. The qualities of this Christian environment, altar-centered and straightforward, proclaimed this faith in unequivocal terms at no better time of the year, as they did on this day, the day of the first impression.

Like a beehive, the faculty was rushing here and there, the drama of the emerging new boy beginning at the crack of dawn with the sound of a lawn mower finishing up last-minute details. In every step, in whatever direction you took, you could hear the sound of rusty hinges and creaking window frames as hibernation officially ended at St. A. for another nine months.

Steven Larue was the perfect roommate and was a take-charge

guy. When we had our first meeting with the boys in the dormitory over whom we were given responsibility, Duck struck with humorous clarity.

The boys were sitting on the floor, most of them with their backs to the wall, hands folded and joined around their knees. The new boys were scared and that was probably good. The old ones knew to be quiet and still. Duck caught their attention instantly.

"Look at me when I'm talking to you," he said pacing, his eyes squinting. Pointing to me, he continued.

"He's the big man. Don't mess with him. If you mess with him, you mess with me. If you mess with me, I'll cut your throat. We're nice guys and we understand how things are. But don't mess with us and don't ever lie to us. Don't ever lie to either one of us. And if we ever, if we ever, catch one of you stealing as much as a pencil, I'll stick that pencil up your ass."

I grinned but knew he was right. I heard the same speech before and my experience taught me the contents of his remarks were dead on target.

"Both Duck and I will check your rooms," I explained. "If you don't know the do's and don'ts, it won't be an excuse, so, you'd better find out what they are. In particular, we'll check everyday to make sure you make your bed up, sweep your floors, empty your trash cans, and flush the toilets, please."

When I finished my delivery, it instantly occurred to me that Sammy and I were going through the same types of days. The first night came to a close with Duck and I checking each room at lights-out, issuing warnings and reminders.

Before I climbed in the bottom bunk between fresh sheets, with Duck snoring above, I read a little and zipped a letter off to Mother. I stepped outside in the warm night air and sat briefly on the steps of Hughson Hall.

"I've got it made in the shade," I said to myself.

CHAPTER 14

The Lumberjack

During the early days of the 1968 school year, I spent free time with Father Hazelton, seeking advice on handling my new responsibilities and just shooting the breeze. He was special to me.

"Billy, I want to speak with you for a moment," my new math teacher, Mr. Allen Sherwin, said.

"Yes, sir," I replied.

"Billy, I know you've had difficulties in math for several years and I want to make you an offer. You have class with me during second period. You also have several periods during the day that you're not really doing anything. I want to suggest getting off to a good start by attending math class twice a day for at least a couple of months . . . just to make sure you get all of the basics down. If you have a good beginning, you'll have a good ending."

"Sure," I said. "I'll do whatever you think is best. I could probably use the extra help."

"Fine. Because I knew you would agree, your schedule has already been changed," he said.

"I'll be there," I said.

I liked math but just passing was a chore. It knew it was going to take two classes to achieve that.

There was now virtually no free time at all. I was always busy doing something, including reading harsh letters from Mother.

In the middle of September, she wrote and was still upset about the money owed at the end of the summer. I wrote her back and did the best I could to reconcile and absolve myself of the crimes I committed.

Dear Mom,

OK. Let's settle things, OK? I know my past actions are unforgivable. I realize I've done wrong because my heart feels it. I feel like leaving this place.

I ask for forgiveness and also ask that this unpleasant happening will not be spoken of again. Never. Because I can't take any more letters like the ones I've been getting. You've gotten the point across more than clear. So please send me a happy letter. Please. I will make up for it. I'm begging for another chance. The money will be repaid.

I love you, Mom, and if it's all right with you, I'd like for us to make a new start. I think Dad would certainly agree to that.

Love,
Billy

There was much less letter writing going on because of this new dimension of responsibility and even Mother wrote and apologized for her sparseness of hellos.

As the seniors' camaraderie deepened, so did our required work. Father Henry was especially demanding in the English class and his nightly reading assignment was on the average of fifty to eighty pages. Weekend assignments were stiffer and reached upwards of a hundred pages. I learned very quickly that if there was one class that I would not attempt to attend unprepared, it was his.

There were eleven of us in his class and it was first period. We sat in two rows that spread horizontally in front of the chalkboard in the new Sherwin building. When any teacher entered the room, we rose quietly and stood perfectly still until we were instructed to sit down.

When he entered the room, my eyes would study every wrinkle, every hair, and every twinge of movement in his body to see what kind of day we were going to have. Only two weeks into the year, we received our first baptism under his commanding presence.

As he often did, he entered grinning, the corners of his buzzard's beak held tightly, so as not to unleash too much joy that could be interpreted for leisure or frivolous class time.

We flew to our feet not wanting to be the last one seen standing who often would be the first one called to answer questions about the previous night's reading. That day, we were studying John Dunne.

Father Henry spent a quarter of an hour on Dunne's style and his eloquence of penmanship when he began slowing down. It was obvious to all of us what was coming.

"In lieu of that analysis, what would you say of Dunne's use of the metaphor, 'blood of innocence,' in *The Flea*?"

He paused, taking aim at his target.

"Mr. Froneburger, what do you think?"

Everybody in that room knew that Hamburger had not read one single page of the assignment, and our heads turned slowly to focus on him and the massacre that was about to occur.

Hamburger paused thoughtfully, his eyes wandering above, probably counting the number of ceiling tile in each row.

As his fear of the inevitable and Father Henry's expectations met at the crossroads, all Hamburger could do was stare and scratch his chin.

Father Henry repeated once again, "Mr. Froneburger, what do you think?"

Hamburger made the fatal mistake of speaking. "Father, I think John Dunne's stupid or something."

When Hamburger spouted out the word "stupid," we knew his life was over.

The Czar cleared the first row of desks like an Olympic hurdler and grabbed him by both sides of his collar and began the confrontation.

"Nobody calls John Dunne stupid and if you do, you better

make sure you've read every single word the man has ever written! Do you think you're going to come into this class completely unprepared and mutter nonsense?"

He ranted and screamed and our hearts went out to Hamburger whose neck and head was going every which of way. The Czar just kept shaking him like a can of shaving cream.

"Don't ever come in this class again with an answer like that or you'll rue the day that you do. Preparation, Mr. Froneberger, preparation!"

When the old man was done, he turned to the rest of us and calmly stated, "Does anybody else have an unprepared contribution they wish to make?"

Not me. I went stone-cold and sank as low as I could in my chair, praying to God that I would not be next. The Czar recovered, found his place at the front of the room, and returned to his previous question.

Crackling sobs could be heard behind me and I dared not allow my attention to be diverted by Hamburger's embarrassment.

The class continued with brilliant and alert discussion of Mr. John Dunne's poetry. All of us were relieved when it was over.

I never went into that class unprepared and that is the reason I did so well under Father Henry's convincing teaching techniques. No one wanted to be on the tail end of those valuable lessons.

Occasionally, there would be a boy who would stand up against such treatment and the results were usually pretty dismal.

It was interesting to watch the dynamics of such a scene play itself out because it happened so rarely that very few faculty members were not completely thrown off balance and sent spinning into searching for an appropriate response.

I would never have in all my dreams considered doing anything less than accepting what punishment rained down upon me, and mending my own bruises as best I could, even if it meant humiliation and rejection.

If I felt a twinge of pride in seeing someone stand up, I, nevertheless, saw the futility of such behavior and did little to encourage it from others. While I may have fantasized about this type of infantile and grandiose rebellion, when that blow of shame came, I retreated once again to the ground, and found little difficulty in reconciling the dream and the reality. Standing up here was making the grade, not bucking it. Bucking it could be bloody.

Everything that had happened to me seemed to have lifted me out of the pit from which I originated and led me with fascinating deception away from my wound and to a height where I did not care to reach down and extinguish its flames. Out of sight, out of mind, I thought.

I chose to believe that who I was, was the president of this, the president of that, the one who performed such and such. I was so remarkably sure of this new identity that I strove at even greater speed toward it and the release it appeared to offer.

I saw myself as having created myself, that I was the great one, the deed itself, and when that happened, I rose like a hot air balloon, not knowing that my flight was finite. There were occasional jolts of recollection that I chose to ignore and disregard. One of them happened very early in the year.

The St. Andrew's student body was self-governing, the seniors being largely responsible for all dormitories and chores that affected every building on campus. Its student council was composed of the prefects and the Headmaster, Father Henry. The council met every Monday night to deal with students who had been charged with minor violations such as stealing, smoking, and failure to complete chores.

The council was rarely given the responsibility of confronting more serious infractions such as drinking or drugs. As a group, we met in private to discuss the charges and the students would then be ushered in to give their side of the story. Afterwards, around the huge, circular, oak table, under the guidance of the Czar, we would decide guilt or innocence and the necessary steps for punishment if found guilty, which was usually the case.

In the later part of September, as the meeting was about to start, Speedy came by to tell us that neither he nor Father Henry would be at the council meeting, and that Mr. Sherwin would be standing in as our advisor.

We had neither objection nor input. Mr. Sherwin showed up several minutes late dressed in his standard bow tie and plaid coat and quickly, the ball got rolling.

"Mr. Brisban, you have heard the charges. What do you have to say?" Mr. Sherwin asked.

"It wasn't my fault. Somebody else gave me the cigarette. I didn't have them with me when I got caught."

"Who gave you the cigarette?" Mr. Sherwin asked.

He paused, wiped the back of his hand across his nose from right to left, and took a deep breath. "Do you really expect me to rat on my friends? Do you think . . ."

Sherwin met him halfway.

"I advise you to guard your mouth, Mr. Brisban, unless, of course, you want to get in more trouble."

"I hate this dump, I don't care what you do," he snarled back, "but get off my back and do what you're going to do."

"This isn't going to be pretty," Bullet whispered to me.

"Nope, it isn't," I replied.

Brisban weighed no more than one hundred pounds soaking wet, had been caught smoking for the third time, and had quickly nailed his coffin shut. He stood resolute, antagonistic, and condemned. We remained quiet, bracing for the worse. And the worse was on its way with Brisban's name on it. This young man would walk the long way tonight.

"I feel I need to oblige you, Mr. Brisban," Mr. Sherwin said, pausing briefly. "So, we'll speed this up. Mr. Brisban, please wait outside," he said, hastily ushering the angry asparagus stalk outside.

Sherwin stepped back in and placed his hands on the table. "Council, what is Mr. Brisban's punishment?" he asked.

Our discussion took on an uncharacteristically divided flavor. Some of the prefects voted for two licks with others arguing for no licks because they didn't feel little Brisban could survive it. Me, I could see the lights coming on in Mr. Sherwin's eyes.

"I don't think he's going to make it here, Mr. Sherwin," Ricky said. "He doesn't really want to be here. I don't think that punishing him is going to help at all. Maybe one of us should talk to him."

Weaver quickly chimed in. "He's been here, what, twice for smoking? This being the third time, I think he should receive what anybody else would receive . . . three licks."

"I don't think he can take three licks," Merch added. "I don't think he's big enough. I think one or two licks would be better."

"I agree," I said. "He's a little guy . . . one or two licks would be better than three."

"Gentlemen, we need to come to a decision. Is it one or two licks?"

Each of us raised our hand indicating the number of licks. Deadlock. The tie vote went to the head prefect.

Weaver's eyes floated around the table. He paused, and said, "I vote for two licks."

Ricky rose and left the room to bring the damned back to us.

Sherwin readied himself as he reached for the paddle and rolled up his shirt sleeves.

"Oh shit," Bullet whispered. "Watch, I bet he gets a good toehold," he whispered to Ricky.

"Mr. Brisban, you are going to receive two licks for your third smoking offense," Sherwin stated.

"I guess I'm supposed to care," Brisban barked back.

"I'll see if I can get you to change your mind," Mr. Sherwin said.

"He just doesn't know when to shut his mouth," Merch whispered to Sammy.

Brisban's arrogance swiftly melted into fear.

"Lean on that chair," Sherwin said, gritting his teeth.

Brisban positioned his hands on the arms of the oak chair and bent over, facing the radiator. Sherwin rearranged his footing to deliver the upcoming blow.

The first swoop was so off it's target, the wood actually moved in sideways instead of flat, and it caught the skinny boy under his buttocks at the top of the back of his legs, causing his body to lurch straight up, hands now displaced to squeeze his legs. He screamed at the top of his lungs.

"Get back down there!" Sherwin yelled, his eyes on fire.

The prisoner grabbed the chair quickly and just in time, too, as the second lick hit with such force that it sent him spiraling over the chair, head first into the radiator which rang out loudly, clanking and vibrating along the whole wall.

Hysteria ruled the moment as Brisban's legs flapped in the air, his body writhing to upright itself.

"And you better not be sent back in here anytime soon!" Mr. Sherwin yelled, his voice echoing above the still rattling radiator.

We sat and stared at one another in disbelief as the boy staggered out of the room, limping. Unaware of our whispers, Sherwin was putting his coat back on, readjusting his clothing and demeanor.

"Damn, I think he crippled him," Fuller said, palming his remark to Sammy.

"Jesus Christ, he took his fucking legs out from under him," I said to Fuller.

"That man is a lumberjack, he's a damn lumberjack," Weaver announced to Limpy who was still under the spell of having witnessed the most memorable paddling we had seen to date.

Sherwin did not mean to do it. I knew that. I knew the paddle must have slipped or Sherwin had lost his balance . . . or something. Something justifiable other than what just happened.

Mr. Sherwin was not a tyrant and was loved by many boys. While this event would not advance his preferred reputation, we chuckled about it, in awe of our substitute paddler and when we kidded him, he launched back with disdain and anger and made it clear that it wasn't a laughing matter.

"Perhaps Mr. Brisban will think twice before winding up back in here," he argued.

"No shit, Sherwin," somebody said quietly without being heard.

That boy would never be the same again and neither was I when it happened to me. I recalled the horror at home of having no choice but to resign myself to the abuse that so cruelly came creeping, like hands commanded to rest on a chair, leaving the body exposed and bare, open to blows of shame and unforgettable torment.

Late at night the door would so slowly open, casting light that spread evenly along the walls and disappear again into darkness, the clicking sound of the doorknob marking and exposing the presence of the intruder.

Beads of sweat gathered so quickly on my forehead, palms dead and white, the tightness of every muscle leaping forward uselessly to form a defenseless wall. Which side of the room is he going to? Mine or his?

My head was fixed on the wall away from the sight of him and his unbounded desire, and only the rustling of my bed covers would jar me from this breathless state, muscles collapsing in defeat, tears held back by years of learning to deny and pretend. I did not fight. I did not struggle. I did not speak. I pushed my pain and rage and hatred as far away from me as I could and stood once again in morning's light in one piece, damning God, and daring the divine sonuvabitch to end it once and for all.

The boy who left that room, with backside burning, fingers wrestling to rub away the pain of his swollen and inflamed skin, probably did the same thing. While I sympathized with him, there was a sigh of relief that it wasn't me. At least my tormentor was dead.

While the tale of Brisban's execution-style punishment was making its way around campus, I quickly forgot the boy's plight and was unsuspecting of the movement of the ashes in my mind.

Outwardly, I was in a trance induced by success but inside, I swam backwards towards a confrontation with my oppressor.

CHAPTER 15

Falling off the Edge

As football unfolded, we got off to a dismal start, getting beat 46-0 in the first game. I enjoyed a starting position on offense and defense but under those conditions, it was more of an embarrassment. I always did the very best I could but my experience with the game was limited so I was nothing to brag about.

I had only a few brilliant moments on defense and spent most of my time chasing people who ran past me. I would occasionally end up with several completed passes, a touchdown once in a blue moon, and my share of unassisted tackles. Entering St. Andrew's weighing about one hundred thirty-five pounds, I was tilting the scales at close to one hundred sixty-five pounds a year later. It hardly enhanced my game. Nonetheless, I had fun.

There was a terribly humiliating experience that occurred in the Chapel Hill game, the very first game, played on our field on a Saturday afternoon. We had received instructions all week long concerning an all-state back who would be our biggest problem and who averaged one hundred fifty-two yards a game the previous year, scoring seventeen touchdowns.

We drilled relentlessly in defense, keying in on his movements, and were well prepared by the end of the week. I don't think it would have mattered if we had drilled at all.

By the end of the game, the score was thirty-nine to nothing and they were not going to let up at all. They marched downfield with under two minutes to go and it was all-state back sweep right, all-state back sweep left, all-state back all the way down the field. On a third down play on our fifteen-yard line, a deaf mute could figure out what was coming next. They had just run a sweep to my right so I positioned myself as middle safety edging to the left, knowing that this might be my last shot at Mr. Touchdown.

When the ball was snapped, it seemed as if their entire line pulled left. My footsteps were moving parallel with this wave of Halloween black and orange and in seconds, there were only two people standing, Mr. Touchdown and me.

As he began sprinting to the sideline, he changed direction to head straight to me. I will never forget the look on his face. He was smiling.

I welcomed this last hit and moved several yards in front of the goal line moving straight to the left hash. As we drew to one another I lowered my head, hoping to break his ankle or take off the lower part of his leg. We met helmet to helmet on the two-yard line.

All I remember is asking myself, "How did he get so low?"

When I stood up, I was one yard out of the end zone, ten yards from where we collided. He stood with ball held high, touchdown number four for him, the crowd going wild. I was laughed off the field.

Now whether or not this discouraging beginning caused my mind to wander, I don't know. But I began thinking of how to get home for a prefect's weekend, a one-time weekend departure granted only to the chosen eight. As September rolled its way through the top of the mountain, Mother wrote to make a similar suggestion.

Billy, I wrote Father Henry today to say if you were doing well enough in your studies, you could come home for a weekend. I can't see where you're going to get the money for a ticket, but this is up to you. Will you not miss a football game? If so, then you should wait until you don't have a game to come. Also, I don't know what you're going to do for money when you get home. Again though, this is up to you, since I've already explained that I have none to spare.

I'm so proud of both of you, and I hope you will take all your responsibilities seriously and do a very good job.

Billy, I think perhaps rather applying to Guilford, it might be better if you substituted the University of North Carolina at Greensboro. It's a better school, and the tuition would be considerably cheaper.

We were close to finishing up our first grading term and there was much talk about Parents Weekend scheduled for early November. We knew that Mother wasn't coming up this year because of the money situation but that presented no problems for Big Sam or me. We were both comfortable and had already settled into a positive, daily routine of study and sports.

There was the usual trouble with some of the boys running away, homesickness being the umbrella term given to all such endeavors. While the morale of the student body always escalated as Parents Weekend neared, it typically would soar downward the week afterwards.

Our collective hearts and souls made up this masculine geography called St. Andrew's, now vertical, now horizontal, and it was always at this time of the year that our academic work was the most stringent, grueling hours spent on John Dunne's poetry rather than familiar landscapes of home.

Father Henry was again articulate and masterful about this crucial time of the year in his communications to the parents.

I urge all of you, especially you parents of new boys, to hold the line and not to give in when and if your boy calls about being homesick and wanting to come home. I can assure you that your son is active and well taken care of and as far as I know has not received any unfair or harsh treatment by anyone concerned.

Some are for the first time growing up to be men, and they are just frankly resisting this process. Many would rather be enjoying the comforts and leisure and extravagances of being home rather than facing the regular routine, the demanding academic requirements, and the overall development of body, mind, and soul that they are finding at this school.

I can assure you that I have seen tremendous strides of development on the part of the new boys, even in a short time of a few weeks. They are responding magnificently to the simple but fulfilling life at St. Andrew's, and I believe that you parents of the new boys will see great changes in them when you come to St. Andrew's for the Parents' Weekend. I believe that your boy is developing in a fine way, and I want you to know that I am happy to share in his development and to have the privilege of being a teacher and guide for him.

I was just about to learn first-hand the deepest of lessons that this man would ever teach me and he would accomplish it with only a few words. My chance came quicker than I thought.

In our second week in October, the football game had suddenly been moved to a Thursday night for an unknown reason. I saw it as my perfect opportunity to take a long, well-deserved weekend, leaving Friday morning, the day after the ball game.

Knowing that I had Mother's permission, it was a simple task of obtaining the Czar's permission.

"Remember, Billy, you will be responsible for your work on Monday."

"Yes, sir, I understand," I replied. "Thank you."

Back in the room, Duck sailed through the door. "C'mon, let's go get Mrs. Tate to open up. I . . ."

"Listen," I said, "I've got talk to you."

"What's going on?" he asked, unalarmed.

"I'm not coming back. I'm not coming back. I'm going to stay at home."

"What? What the fuck are you talking about?" he asked.

"I want to go home, I'm tired of doing all of this all of the time. I can't . . ."

"I can't believe you're saying this! This is insane. You can't go home 'cause there's no home for you to go back to. You think there is but there ain't. I know 'cause I tried this shit my second year here. Man, once you're gone, you're gone, and there's no going back. Does Sam know what you're doing?"

"No, I haven't told him. He doesn't know and don't tell him either. He might call Mother."

"I won't let you! I'll tell the Czar myself!" he threatened.

"You won't tell anybody and besides, if I'm gone, you'll have the room to yourself."

"Fuck you, I don't want the fucking room, you dipwad! I want you to stay."

"I already sold a lot of my stuff . . . my records and stuff to buy a one-way ticket when I get to Chattanooga."

"You're an egghead." he said. "Tell me who bought the stuff and I'll get it back after I break their fucking neck!"

"Duck, I've got to go. I just can't stay here anymore."

He crawled up to his bed and lay down. His back turned away from me as I straightened my desk.

Maybe I was just too happy there and felt a need to sabotage the success I was experiencing. Maybe destroying the only environment that truly made a difference in my life was important to me. I cannot say that I will ever understand why I made that decision, but I did.

Night after night Duck and I mulled over my resolution and he did his best to talk me out of it. But the dye was cast.

When a situation like this presented itself, it was a time for everyone to make or lose some extra money. Dumbrowsky, the senior bookie, handled all of the bets. And there was a bundle of money on the line. Will he or won't he go over the hill? I said I was. Few believed me.

Gone were my records, clothes, dictionary, American flag, hand mirror, baseball cards, two copies of Playboy, my letter jacket, two pairs of shoes, and three UNC T-shirts. Having

sold everything I owned and emptying out what was left of my
bank account, I amassed enough loot to buy a one-way plane
ticket home from the Chattanooga airport. I called, made
reservations, and waited.

Because of the sale of everything in my room, the bets shifted
the other way and most believed at that point that my plan would
be completed. I certainly had no doubt.

Sammy was undisturbed by it all but would grab me and hit
me, slap my head lightly, or bear-hug me from behind and say,
"You're so stupid, Billy. You take things too personally."

"You don't know how I feel, Sammy. You don't know what I'm
going through."

"I've always known what you're going through. The difference
between you and me is that I don't go there. It's the past, Billy,
and the sooner you learn that, the sooner you're going to be able to
let it go. Can you really say that you want to go home? Home to
what? Home to the very thing that brought us here in the first
place? Jesus, just think about it."

"I can't just forget it. I try and it doesn't work. I try." I said.
"I'm just not as strong as you are."

He tried to talk me out of it a million times over. I didn't listen
to him or anyone else.

With the fanfare and talk of my official getaway, I worried
about being discovered before I had the chance to make a run for
it. But Thursday night came swiftly and with no mention of my
sinister plot by Father Henry, Speedy, Father Hazelton, or Mr. Gautier.

The game was hardly important to me but we fought diligently
and salvaged a respectful fourteen to seven loss. Consequently, I
felt upbeat and ready.

"What are you going to do when you get home?" Wreck asked.

"I guess I'll enroll in the local high school. I guess I'll stay at
home."

"What if your mother doesn't let you stay at home?" the
President asked.

"I'll figure something out."

"I can tell you right now," Sammy announced to the group,

"our mother is not going to let him stay at home. She'll kill him before she lets him stay at home."

"If the Czar finds out what you're doing, he'll kill you first," Duck warned.

"Thanks for your support," I said.

The evening was spent with several of my closest friends in my room till well past lights-out. I had been in the process of saying my goodbyes to the rest of the crew all during the week and these last moments were good ones. The talk was about girlfriends, home, term papers, faculty members, and food.

"Billy, take care, man. See ya' around," Hatch said.

"Later, Billy," Flat Tire said, shaking my hand.

The goodbyes soon tailed off and one by one, they left to return to their own rooms, the sounds of their slippers sliding along the waxed hallway in rhythmic cadence as I slithered in my bottom bunk for the last time.

I tried to calculate the memories, the people, the scents, and trials of my time spent at St. Andrew's. It was a barrage of voices, sounds, colors, faces, and words which burned inside of me, but it was as though there another force this night, something vaguely identifiable but invisible that lurked in that room.

It was neither uncomfortable nor disturbing. It had a weight because I felt it in my stomach. It had a sound because I could hear it in my heart.

When the alarm went off, it was five o'clock Friday morning. I dressed hurriedly and raced across the black asphalt sidewalk with suitcase bouncing to meet Father Hazelton. He was there in the idling school van, clouds of exhaust billowing out into an already foggy, October mountain morning.

We greeted one another warmly and off we went. I stared out for the last time across a campus whose buildings I could not see, whose trees were veiled, and whose life lay hidden behind the screen of moist gray. I did not look back.

In customary dress, I was wearing proper slacks, hard-soled shoes, a tie and my school blazer. In ten minutes we were at the I-

24 on-ramp where Father Hazelton let me out. I would hitch-hike the remainder of the trip.

"Billy, have a safe trip but be careful in this fog. You may have difficulty getting a ride for a while but one will come. God bless you."

"God bless you, too, Father Hazelton, and thanks for the lift."

As he pulled the van into drive to pull away, the brakes lights suddenly popped on. He backed up slowly, rolled the window down and prophetically said, "Did you forget anything?"

"No, sir. I've got what I need here," pointing to my near empty suitcase.

"Are you sure?" he asked, peering through my nervousness.

"Yes, sir, I'm fine," I replied.

"Billy, are you all right?"

"Yes, sir."

"Then, I'll see you Sunday afternoon, correct?"

"Yes, sir, Sunday afternoon."

Smiling, he stared at me for a moment and off he drove. I ran down the ramp to hitchhike to Chattanooga.

In an hour and a half, I was riding past Lookout Mountain and the lights of the city were in view. I got out of the truck and jogged to a gas station to call a taxi that got me to the airport by eight fifteen. My aerial escape was scheduled for nine thirty-seven.

I spent the remaining hour as a fugitive, fearing that Father Hazelton had discovered my plan. I imagined a school van driven by a mad priest screaming into the airport before I had time to disappear.

I enjoyed this flight from my tightly scheduled life at St. Andrew's and found substance in the childish courage I was now displaying, regardless of how irresponsible and fruitless it may have really been. I was only convinced that what I was doing was the right thing to do.

After arriving in Charlotte, I hitched down to Monroe, and by two thirty that afternoon, stepped through Mother's front door. The conversation was lukewarm and she was patiently waiting for a financial explanation of how I intended to spend the rest of the weekend without asking her for money.

"Tomorrow, I'll be getting a job," I said not wanting to deal with her.

"Why a job for one day? What good will that do?"

And then I said it.

"I'm not going back."

"You're not going back to what?" she demanded.

"I said, I'm not going back." I was using my hands to talk. "I'm going to stay here and go to school in Monroe."

"Oh no, you're not! You're not doing this to me and you're not doing it to yourself!" she screamed.

"I'm old enough to make decisions for myself. I've decided to stay here."

"Not in this house you're not!" she screamed.

She stormed back into the bedroom where I could hear her begin to cry. I brushed the remarks off as part of the hell I would have to temporarily endure and left the house to go down to the lake.

I returned late that night to find the door locked and was unable to get in or bring her to the door. I decided to sleep in the car. Cramped and cold I was too exhausted to go anywhere else.

I hitched down to the store the next morning, got a bite to eat, hitched back where I walked several hours around the lake, and tried once again to get into the house. This time she came to the door and I was let in, a glacial glare governing the crisis in which she did not speak to me but removed herself from my presence for several more hours in her locked bedroom.

It was getting close to lunchtime when she stomped into the living room and informed me that I had a telephone call. I was sure it was a friend with whom I could escape this parental hell.

"Hello?" I said, answering enthusiastically.

"Hello, Billy! How's your weekend going?"

It was Father Henry.

"It's fine, Father. How are you?"

"Well, Billy, things here are fine. I had a little difficulty last night with a few issues because, funny thing, Billy, there was a rumor that you had gone over the hill and that you would not be returning. I did the best I could to convince the boys and teachers who were concerned that that simply wasn't the case, that you had applied for and had been given a prefect's weekend, and that you would be back Sunday afternoon."

I said nothing.

"How is your mother? Is she well?"

"Yes, sir, she is fine. Everything is fine."

"That's splendid. By the way, what time does your plane arrive in Chattanooga on Sunday?"

"Father, I don't know."

"Would you be kind enough to call me back shortly to give me that information and I will have Father Hazelton pick you up at the airport."

I said nothing. I couldn't say anything. My throat was choked. The tears were welling up.

"I must admit, Billy, the boys were very clever. They must have hidden all of your belongings because your room looked abandoned. Even your letter jacket was missing and I know how much that means to you. But I was not worried and I told the boys, 'Don't worry, Billy McNeal will be back.'"

I said nothing.

"I told the boys you would be back because you would never deceive me or the school in such a way because you are a man of your word and you can be trusted. You told me just about a year ago that you were a man of your word when I caught you sneaking down the fire escape. And over the course of that year, you taught me that that was who you were. You were given a prefectship because of that. You were given a prefectship because you had integrity, because you lived up to your word. I do not expect any less from you in these circumstances. You made an agreement with me about this weekend and about your return to school."

There was silence. And with a brief, contemplative pause, without really knowing what to say, I replied, "That's right, Father. I'll be back Sunday afternoon. I just don't know when the plane leaves."

I was lost in a barrage of emotions.

"That's nothing less than what I told the boys. That's good, Billy. We'll be happy to have you back with us tomorrow. Billy, would you be able to settle that matter within the hour, so that we have that information today? It would be very helpful and we would avoid a possible mix-up."

"Yes, sir. I'll call back within the hour."

"Thank you Billy. I hope your weekend goes well."

"Thank you, Father. I hope yours does, too."

"It's going just fine, Billy. Thank you. See you tomorrow. And Billy, if you need anything, please call me personally."

"OK. I will. Goodbye, Father."

"Goodbye."

I walked to my room and plopped my face in my pillow. I cried until my eyes were swollen and my vision was blurred. I angrily went to Mother's bedroom.

"I don't have any money to buy a ticket!" I said glaring at her, wanting a fight.

Combatively she shouted, "What do you expect me to do? You created this disaster, now, you figure it out!"

I ended up calling Uncle Charlie, explaining the situation, and he agreed to pay for the ticket. But he made it clear he wasn't happy about it.

The next day Uncle C escorted me all the way not just to the airport, but through the airplane door and to my seat, checking once again before walking out of the exit to confirm I was still there.

When I arrived at the Chattanooga airport around five thirty, Father Hazelton was waiting there for me and surprisingly, he said nothing, but smiled in an understanding manner.

As we walked to the baggage pick-up, he put his arm around me, held me tightly around my shoulder, and supported my now, emotionally drained body.

"Perhaps, when you're ready, we could have a talk," he said.

"If it's OK, I'd rather not talk about it tonight. Would it be all right if I came to see you another time?" I asked.

"Of course," he said, patting me on the back.

The ride back to the mountain was completely silent and he did not attempt to intrude in my pain. Were it not for the sounds of the van's loud engine, its tires whining, holding on to the curves of the Monteagle Mountain hills, it would have been easy for me to have pretended that I had died for I was lifeless, graveyard still, hollow, and incapable of any movement or sound.

Father Henry's voice was breathing in me and I understood why I chose to return. I wanted to live up to his expectations. I wanted his approval, his blessing, his love, and knew instinctively, although the words do not come to a seventeen-year-old boy, that it was important for me to live up to my word, for he had kept his, and had protected me from another harsh punishment a year before. I wanted his respect.

When the van reached the sight of the Holiday Inn, there was a surge in my chest that I desperately tried to contain. I tightened my throat and crushed the muscles of my stomach inward to lock down the tears that were fighting their way up and out.

When I could struggle no more, I began sobbing, placing my head on Father Hazelton's leg, my limp right hand resting on his knee. He stroked my head and wiped my tears across my cheek as we drove slowly across the interstate bridge and back to school. Once the van made its patented turn into the school's entrance, he stopped.

"I want you to know that I love you so very much and that I understand. I cannot take your pain from you but I can be here for you and with you. Billy, I so deeply understand and I am sorry that you feel like this. I know you'll be fine."

I continued sobbing, heaving, squeezing his knee, dying inside as he remained close to me, waiting patiently until I could go on.

"But I'm not happy and I don't know how to be happy," I said. "I try and I do everything I can to make everybody else happy and it still doesn't work . . . I just don't know what to do."

My voice trailed off into more tears.

"There is inside of each of us, Billy, a haven, a center that has the ability to lead us through times like this. It knows what you should do and how to get there. You are young and impatient, and just don't know yet. Don't be deceived. It is a life journey and it takes time. You are strong and you will grow through this time in your life and you will see more and more and more." He paused.

"Let me tell you a story," he continued.

My tears and sobbing were slowing.

"When I was in seminary, one of the professors enjoyed telling me this story and I will share it with you. He used to always say that God was closer to those who made mistakes than those who were holy. This is what he said. He said that God in Heaven holds each of us by a silver thread. When we are in pain, when we make a mistake, we cut the thread. So God ties the two ends together again, making a little knot, bringing us closer and closer each time back to Him. Many, many, times in your life, will you cut the thread and each time it will be mended until the moment comes when you find yourself with Him. Each time you will lift your head back up, to try again, again, and again. Each time you will bridge the distance between yourself and your goal. But Billy, you must never quit. Never quit. Never. The struggle will provide you the foundation to build your life. Do you remember when you were on Shuford's Hill? Do you remember when you didn't think you could go on any longer?"

"Yes, sir. I remember," I said, a smile emerging through my tears. "How could I ever forget the hill?"

"Billy, this is just another hill. It's just another kind of hill. You have what it takes. The question is, will you use it?"

I did not reply immediately but paused. "Thank you for the ride. I appreciate not having to hitchhike back."

"You are quite welcome."

The quieting of my breathing was occurring simultaneously with the release of tightness in my arms and chest. Some relief had descended and I was ready to exit the van to return to my room and the life that I attempted to leave.

As I went to the side of the van to get my suitcase, Father Hazelton met me there.

Eye to eye, he put his hands on my shoulders and said, "Teaching only takes place when learning does. Thank you for teaching me. You know where I am if you need me."

I hugged him and was becoming emotional again. "I don't understand what you said just then."

"You will . . . you will. Don't worry anymore right now. You've had a trying day and you need some rest."

As he moved away from me to leave, I turned to him.

"Father Hazelton, something happened to me when I was young. There's something I want to tell you, but I don't know if I can tell you tonight," I said.

"I understand. You can tell me when you're ready. That is why I am here. It's what I do. Just let me know when you want to talk."

"OK . . . I will," I said.

We both smiled and he disappeared as the van crept out of sight around the gravel bend at St. Dominic's.

I left my suitcase at the now empty, night-covered quad and hands in pockets, I went to the lake where I lay in the grass watching the stars begin to appear, the purple darkening to black.

Wrestling with this experience, I plodded inch by inch through this regrettable weekend. Before I finally returned to my room, I sat once more by the mirror-still waters whose cattails hid my presence.

When I finally dried my eyes and wiped my runny nose on my skirt sleeve, it was just in time to check in for lights-out.

CHAPTER 16

Welcome Back

Dumbrowsky was pissed. And so were a lot of other guys when they were informed of my arrival. Dumbrowsky ended up owing a lot of money and was a clear-cut loser in the whole adventure. Sammy never recanted his firm belief that I would come back and he made out pretty well on most of his bets.

He had said to everyone, "Oh, I don't doubt he's going home but there ain't no doubt that Momma's going to send his butt back up here either."

Having borrowed some additional money from Uncle Charlie, the school bank, and Duck, I went about buying back as many of my belongings as possible.

Father Henry did not mention his knowledge of what truly transpired and when I reported to class on Monday morning, he was genuinely courteous and gracious to me as though nothing happened.

As far as he was concerned, I was on an official weekend leave and reported back to school as required. There was little doubt in my mind that Father Hazelton shared with him all that took place between the two of us but the Czar did not bring it up. Instead, we got back to work.

I struggled to convey to Mother what I had been through and why this frantic episode had occurred but made little sense.

Mom,

    I'm in a senseless dream, it seems, and I want to talk

about life and such. No one else in the world seems to understand my thoughts.

I don't know what to say about the stunt I pulled. When a person is crying and feels low, does that necessarily mean that he's not happy? I've been sad but yet, I'm happy. I've got a good life to live. I've got a home, a good one and people who care about me. I've got so much but I don't realize it. The most important thing I can do is to love and receive love in return. I think I'd rather be poor without a home just as long as I held love in my heart and knew that there was someone else in the world that cared about me.

I picture myself walking by the sea with my hands in my pocket, my head staring at different things and it seems like whatever I dream or even think about, there's music in the background . . . the kind that makes you realize stuff. There's a thousand things running around in my mind that seem very obscure but yet, it's like I've felt them before and I feel like I have answers for them somewhere. But when I think of them individually, I can't tell what the answer is or what is going to happen in the end.

Like, well, take school. I love school but I hate it. I like to study but I hate it. I want to go to college but I don't. I'd like to travel to California and get the first plane to Hawaii and live. When I come home, I act like I hate it, but I can't stand being away from it. I can't stand being away from the people I love.

I don't want to grow up. I'm afraid of paying taxes, buying a house one day, looking for a real job, and about everything else. I want to face life while I'm young. Do you realize in seventeen years, I'll be an old man just about? I'm scared of dying and it seems that it's not too far away. In the next few years, I'll be married, be a father, be a lieutenant in the army, be a college chaplain . . . it's just so confusing. I don't know what I want to be.

And if I do have a son, I sure hope that I don't give him the same answers to his questions that I'm giving you.

I feel like I'm stuck in a boat that's just floating around
an island called Nowhere. I've got to go. I love you, Mom.

———————————

Homecoming was approaching and we were playing SMA again,
our arch-enemy. I was not enthusiastic about the game because of
their strength and record, but looked forward to getting one more
chance to hurt a couple of Gimps.

During the week prior to Homecoming, there was a special
assembly called and as best any of us could tell, it had to do with
some wrongdoing or infraction that had taken place. We were held
fifteen minutes late, spilling over into the instructional time of
first period. That was a rarity of sorts so it was easy to see that
whatever it was, it was important.

The crowd of 160 boys was never still, reverberating with loud
talking and laughing. When the B-Czar stepped through the door,
it fell to an immediate silence.

"Gentlemen, please let me have your attention. Let me have
your attention."

He paused and let his eyes wander the ocean of faces for anyone
still yapping away. We all became respectfully still.

"Gentlemen, it seems we have a problem. It seems that the
gong in the bell tower is missing. It was discovered yesterday when
the tennis team went to celebrate their victory over CHMA."

It was customary at St. Andrew's that whenever a team won, it
notified the entire campus by ringing the chapel bell. But the
chapel bell not having a gong was like King not having a Kong and
the Czar was visibly upset. He continued, pacing the platform
nervously.

"We have reason to believe that some cadets from SMA . . .,"
and with those words, unable to finish, a verdict of guilty was
issued forth from the students in front of him, now leaning forward,
hands on the chairs in front of them. He spoke above them loudly.

"We have reason to believe that some cadets from SMA found
their way into the chapel, wormed their way up to the bell tower,

and stole it. We cannot immediately confirm this but have strong suspicions that this is exactly what took place."

"Why, those sorry mother-fuckers!" the President whispered to everyone on his left.

"That's so damn stupid, I mean, like what are they going to do with a clapper anyway?" Eddie Witt whined.

"Hey, Nitwitt, shut up, you idiot," Weaver said.

Immediately, seven sets of eyes rested on this little fourth former who found himself walking in the wrong part of the woods.

"Hey, a-hole," Duck said, pointing his finger at him, his jaws tightly compressed together, "you just got all the toilets for the rest of the week . . . now, shut up."

Eddie Witt and his brother, Freddie, were two sophomore brothers who were nice guys but who were tagged early as Nitwitt and Dimwitt respectively. Nitwitt had no recourse in this situation but to survive by turning away from Duck and minding his own business.

"Now, boys," the Czar continued, "I don't know what we're going to do about this, but I can tell you this. By God, we are going to get it back!"

And with those words, he made a fist that he threw out at the student body, his body's weight carrying him that much closer to us. A roar ignited among the boys and there were books banging on desks and feet stomping on the floor.

"Get the Gimps! Get the Gimps!" came the battle cry, all of us joining in unison. It shifted in seconds to, "Kill the Gimps! Kill the Gimps!" Getting them wouldn't be enough. Killing them would.

Whatever the old man had in mind, he didn't share it with us and we left for class with morale having soared thirty degrees hotter with just a few simple words. As the week unfolded, the mystery only deepened.

The next night, some of the St. A. boys were caught on the SMA campus about five miles away at two o'clock in the morning and returned to the school by Father James Douglas, the headmaster of the academy. Apparently, the St. A. vigilantes were going through some of the dormitories trying to figure out where that gong was.

When it was announced the next morning what transpired during the night, Father Henry asked that the boys stand up during assembly. There were six of them, all seniors. Bark, Big Sam, Limpy, Yates, Hatch, and Robo I.

"Understand me well on this point, gentlemen, this is serious business," he said loudly, wandering back and forth across the stage. "There will be no more midnight journeys to the academy and if they occur, the punishment will be severe. As for the six seniors who violated virtually every rule in their code of behavior by leaving campus without permission, I have only one thing to say."

He stopped, turned his back to us, his chin in his right hand. We were paralyzed, breathless, waiting for the ax to fall.

He swung swiftly around, pointed his finger at each one of them and said, "Damn good try!"

It was an organized riot. Shouting, screaming, jumping up and down, fists shaking, and hearts exploding!

"You tell 'em, Father!" came the response.

"That sonuvabitch is tough but he's cool," Bullet explained to a group of us.

"You got to hand it to him, he hates those bastards as much as we do," Droo said.

On Friday morning, the day before the game, rumors were riveting around the dorm that something happened the night before, that there were injuries in a fight when some of the St. A. boys caught some Gimps who crept on campus after midnight. Some said that the police were involved and this was the biggest deal since Jesus Christ was seen at the soccer match the year before.

When the assembly was called, there was no Father Henry, and we waited and waited and waited. Thirty minutes later, no Czar. Forty-five minutes later, no Czar. One hour later, no Czar. This was big.

Finally, an hour and a half later, in he bounded, one hand on each side of the entrance, slamming the two doors against the door stops on the concrete block wall, only to have them rebound back again in his hands. He pushed again, forcefully marching his way through.

He was unshaven, unshowered, dressed in blue jeans and tennis shoes, sporting an untucked, bright-red flannel shirt. Most noticeably, he had a glare in his eyes that would have stopped an eighteen-wheeler. He had no more placed his first foot on the first step than he pulled out from under his shirt the chapel clapper which he began waving madly about his head, the student body going berserk.

"I got it, boys! By God, there's going to be some bell ringing tomorrow!" he said, optimistic about tomorrow's big game.

"But that isn't all, boys! I found the ones who stole it and they are here to issue an apology. There are to be no comments made to them whatsoever. Do you understand?" We nodded in unison. "Do you understand?"

And moments later, they marched in. Four cadets in full-dress uniform, shoulder to shoulder through the doors.

The cadets, decked out in their sparkling, army blues and sashes, settled in front of the student body. One of them stepped forward.

"On behalf of the entire student body and faculty of Sewanee Military Academy, I want to apologize for our misconduct and unsportsmanlike behavior. We deeply regret our wrongdoing."

Dignified, well rehearsed, and brief, the lead cadet turned to join the ranks and exit together this roman arena in which they had been spared the true deserved sentence of death.

As soon as the coattail of the last cadet slipped through the door, we erupted again, unified, vocal, and aggressive.

Father Henry was visibly proud of himself and we were every bit as proud of him. He had stepped out from behind the lectern to become one of us, to live our feelings, to breathe our pneuma, and to walk our walk. On that day he built a bridge for a large number of boys who crossed over many times through the years.

Unfortunately, the next day's game was close to a repeat of the game the year before. We were beaten by fifteen points and never got close.

"Bill, don't forget, you've got outside coverage. Stay outside!" Stevenson bellowed.

I was only a few feet from him. I nodded.

When the ball bounced over the deep back's head and was spinning around near the goal line, everyone broke rank.

"Ball!" everyone yelled.

Ignoring my instructions, I left my position to go after the ball. As I ran to the left and headed for the center of the field, a gimp picked up the ball as I was on about the six or seven yard line and headed further to my right to get away from me.

Suddenly, my left leg was limp like a noodle and pain was searing through my body. I was taken off the field, unable to walk, and was placed on the sideline.

The following day I was taken to the Sewanee Hospital where the standard set of X-rays were done. My football days were over.

"Billy McNeal, I am Dr. Ravenel. How are you?"

"I'm fine. I have a lot of pain. My leg doesn't feel so good."

"Your leg is going to be fine. It will take some time. But tell me, how did you hurt your ankle?"

"What ankle?" I asked.

"Your right ankle," he said.

"Oh, that. I was about twelve or thirteen and riding my bike when a dog jumped out at me from behind some bushes and I never saw him coming. It scared me pretty good and caused me to jerk the bike and when I did, I hit a log that was sticking out from a trash pile of brush and when I came to, I was lying in the road with my right foot driven up into the chain and the sprocket. I couldn't get it loose so I just lay there screaming for a while. Somebody finally found me and they took me to the doctor. My mother said it was just something I had to learn to live with."

"Your ankle needs some work as well. I am going to recommend to your mother that we take a closer look at it."

I was back at school by Sunday afternoon and missed no classes at all. Although there was much less letter writing during this second year and Mother complained about it, she did write in early December.

Dear Boys,

I have a minute while waiting for the new listings to come in, but I'm too late to begin writing separate letters and will just send you each a copy. Hope you had a good time in Charleston over the weekend, Sammy. Write me about your trip if you have time.

Billy, I hope you are taking your exercise and working on getting your knee straightened out. These things just do take time and many times an operation is not necessary.

I do hope you have both resolved to spend these last weeks before Christmas studying because your grades indicate that there is plenty of room for improvement. I'm afraid you are both going to be disappointed about college this fall unless you are willing to put forth some extra effort as far as your work is concerned, and there is not going to be one thing to do about it when your final grades are in. You either realize once and for all how important this last year is or just forget it. I'm not even fussing now because it's entirely up to you whether you get into another school from there or not, and it's no longer my responsibility.

I finally got around to responding to Mother's letter two weeks later.

Mom,

Your life has been a very hard one, one not too many people could possibly go through it. The sacrifices you have made for Sammy and me are too numerous to count, and yet, I have given nothing in return except maybe a lot of disappointment and worrying. I think of myself as a burden but know someday, I'll make up for it. I guess Aunt Evelyn told you I called and I feel very guilty and ashamed of the crap I've given you. I really can't explain it. I want to have a perfectly happy Christmas and I know it's going to take more on my part than it will on yours.

First of all, I promise, I won't say I don't want to come back. That's a promise. Secondly, you're going to see some shining grades after Christmas. I'm sorry I've goofed off so much. No excuse. But you'll see a 100 percent improvement. Promise.

I know it's hard for you to walk into the house and find nobody there but you need not cry. You have two fine sons to be proud of and to depend on. I promise I'll change. Life's a hard thing to figure out, but you need to have a small state of rebellion to figure it out, to see if you can make it on your own at the age of seventeen. I see that now.

Of the two of us, I guess I have failed the most, yet, I don't feel ashamed. Failing in this case is still good, I guess. But my standards are getting higher. I have set goals before and stayed with them. Like basketball. I made it, Mom. I was where I had dreamed of being for those three years but then I got creamed on the field and I saw that dream slowly disappear, knowing it may never return and that it may be something I just have to live with. Yet, I don't give up. I play basketball, though the knee is painful and feels like a knife is being stuck in it. The doctor gave strict orders for me not to run, jump or squat. But I didn't put in three years of hard work for nothing.

Well, I promise I'll develop the same idea about my grades. I've thought about after a year in North Carolina, I might want to study law, maybe at Vanderbilt. I want Christmas to be a happy one, one we'll both remember. But understand me as a kid who always meant good but just got caught in the middle of things. Mom, let's have a good Christmas.

I did not know that in believing that there are just some things you have to live with, it is the same thing as saying that there are just some things that you have to live without. It's really not so difficult to understand that people incarcerate themselves for a lifetime because they don't know that they don't know.

CHAPTER 17

Hooded Men and the Last Winter

The winter of our last year at St. Andrew's was a demanding one, surrounded with ice and cold, and was such that the sun disappeared for four months. Forced inside for most of our free time, a kind of emotional impotence was lurking about. There was little to do outside in the cold and yet, there was nothing more useless and futile than sitting around ruminating about home, for such thoughts brought on instant moods of depression and withdrawal.

When I found myself caught up in the webs of the past and overwhelmed with intense longing, I enjoyed taking solitary walks, however brief, out to Piney Point, a mountain-top view of the valley below Sewanee, looking out toward Tullahoma and Shelbyville. Sitting there on the ledge, I enjoyed pitching rocks and dead leaves that would be caught by the winter wind and sail off beyond my sight.

Alone on Piney Point, I felt at ease here in the quiet of the cliff, embraced by the sudden, icy gusts from the valley below.

One Saturday afternoon, I bundled up in my winter clothes and rambled out to the Point with a battery-operated, transistor radio I borrowed from Limpy.

I sat out there, lying on my back, listening to the music when I heard footsteps behind me. I alertly rolled over to see who or what it was, as I was positioned dangerously close to the edge. It was Father Hazelton.

"Beautiful view, isn't it?"

Both of us were scanning the other side of the mountain toward the Sewanee golf course, and watching a soaring red-tailed hawk navigate his way effortlessly among the cliffs.

"Yes, it is, Father. I love it here."

"I saw you walking down by the track and figured that you might be headed this way. Do you mind if I join you?"

"No, of course not. It's fine with me."

Being alone with him was rewarding. He was an easy man to be around.

"What are you thinking about?" he inquired.

"I don't know. Everything, I guess."

"Have you made up your mind about college?"

"Not yet. I've got four applications in. I ought to be accepted somewhere," I said.

"Is there one particular thing that is bothering you?" he asked. "You told me once that there was something that happened to you."

There was a moment of silence.

"It's just that sometimes," I began slowly, "sometimes I feel real alone, like I've got to go through all this stuff myself, that if I don't work hard and be the best, that I'm not going to make it, that I'm going to drown."

"Drown in what?"

"I don't know . . . that I won't succeed."

"Succeed at what?"

"I have no idea. I don't know what I want to do or study in college."

"Billy, what does your heart tell you? Deep inside, what do you want to do?" he asked.

"I don't know Father. Sometimes I don't think I'll ever know. I mean, how do you decide that? Do you just get lucky? Does God drop down out of the sky and tell you?"

"What do you think?" he asked.

"I don't know. It's like there are two people living inside of me, one of them I like, one of them I don't, and I don't know which one is me."

"Which one does your heart tell you is you?"

His eyebrows were slightly raised.

"What do you mean by my heart? That's confusing to me. Is that the same thing as my conscience?"

"Your heart is the voice of God inside of you, a center away from the storm, a place where you can be yourself with all your flaws and problems and feel love and acceptance from God, and know that you have a reason for being here."

"I wish I knew what my reason was . . . but if the question is, what does my heart tell me, then my heart doesn't know. I feel so messed up some of the time."

There was a pause and I began to feel some discomfort.

I asked, "What's your reason for being here, Father?"

"Do you mean here with you?" he said with a smile.

"No, I mean for being alive, for being on this earth?"

"My answer is the same as before when I brought you back from the airport when you considered going over the hill. Being here with you right now."

"So, apparently, you know all the details about that trip?" I asked.

I turned this time to look in the eyes of this wise man and to feel the magnetic attraction once again that I felt for him.

"Yes," he said. "I knew when I let you out on the interstate to hitchhike to Chattanooga."

"Why didn't you try to stop me?" I asked.

"There was no reason to. I trust the process. You were, as you are now, coming to terms with something in your life and it's not up to me to decide what the best way to do that is. I also trust you, Billy. I trust you'll make the best decision. That's why I knew you would come back."

I did not reply but paused and gathered my thoughts.

"But why?" I asked. "How do you know that being with us is your reason for being here on earth?"

"Billy, right now, it's here with you. Tonight, it might be with James or Andrew, to talk, to share, to help guide all of you as best I can, in helping you become what you're capable of becoming, what you want to be. I am here on this earth to serve, to serve you, Jim, Mitch, and all of the others because in doing that, I am serving myself, and my heart, and the voice of God that speaks inside of me."

"But I can't find that place, Father, and I don't know where I'm really going. I have no clue as to how I am supposed to grow up."

I felt my bottom lip began to quiver and there was little need in fighting back the tears. I felt so stupid crying again, girlish and weak. He did not hold me this time but let me remain open to the wind and the cold that swirled and embraced both of us.

"That place, Billy, is inside of you. It is not in a deed and yet, there are things to be done. It is not in words, and yet, there are things to be said. But it first must be sought and yet, it is not going to be found in this world."

"I don't understand that."

"I guess what I'm saying is that you will learn the most when you are still and you open your heart . . . just try to let go of all of your thinking about the past . . . just let things be without feeling the need to react to them. It's like thinking about your girlfriend . . . suddenly you find yourself thinking about her . . . there wasn't anything that really provoked your thinking . . . it just happened. But instead of getting caught up in it and getting depressed, just be aware of it. Just be aware that that's what you're thinking. Don't react to it. Just be aware of it."

There was silence again.

"For example . . . just relax and notice the views . . . be aware of where your thinking is taking you . . . don't do anything about it . . . just notice it. But each time your mind goes somewhere else, bring it back to here, right now, just noticing the view . . . just breathing the mountain air."

We sat there in the hush of winter, fixed and undisturbed. I relaxed again and every time my mind raced to somewhere else, I came back to here.

As the minutes passed, he asked, "So, which one is you? Is it the one that is thinking or the one who is bringing your thinking back to here?"

"It's the one that brings my thinking back to here. That's the one that decides."

"So, when your thinking is out of control, which one are you?

"Then, I'm not me," I interrupted.

"That's right. So, now, you have another and bigger problem than the one you thought you had. You now get to decide which one of the two you want to be . . . at any given moment . . . it's up to you. You can be dishonest or you can live with integrity. You can be loving or you can be unkind. But the problem you have is that now, you know which one of the two you are. And that's not easy. That takes courage. You now know there are no excuses . . . even if you have a good reason . . . there are no excuses. When you are not person you want to be and you want to blame it on someone else, you now know that it is an excuse. It is a technique the mind has for avoiding responsibility, for blaming someone else for what has gone wrong in our life."

"But there are mean, hateful people who do bad things to other people," I said.

"Yes, there are," he replied. "But you will notice that you're still stuck with the problem . . . the problem of choice . . . the problem of taking responsibility for how you feel . . . the problem of becoming your best . . . the you who you know you are, deep down inside."

"I know deep inside that I'm OK, that I'm going to be fine, that I'll figure out what I want to be when I grow up one way or another. I know deep down inside that I'm not afraid."

"When was the last time you felt afraid?" he asked.

"As soon as I saw you."

"And did you go into the fear or did you choose something else?"

"I chose something else. I knew there was no reason to be afraid. You've never given me any reason to be afraid of you."

"Going through your fear will lead you to your faith," he whispered.

As the wind swirled around Piney Point, there was food that passed from him to me. I felt able.

As our discussion dissipated, it was replaced with some humorous, almost irreverent talk about women, work, and about life. Father Hazelton did not try to tame me, to bleed me of my desire to make noise, to roar, to stamp my feet, and fumble my own way through life, but to encourage me, laugh with me, and accept me as I was. Just as I was.

We left together and walked back to school paying attention to raccoon and deer tracks, throwing rocks along the way at targets impossible to hit. He had become an umbilical cord for me and seemed to know just when to move closer and when to back away without abandoning me. His presence lessened my need to suffer.

"So, how is your leg?" he asked.

"It's fine. The doctor says I can play basketball when I come back from Christmas vacation. I wish I didn't have to wait."

"Mending can take time," he said. "You will be fine."

After Christmas vacation, there was very little communication that took place between Mother and us upon our return to school. Christmas hibernation came without warning.

The holidays passed uneventfully with most of our energy directed toward the upcoming exams and the last semester in which I did manage to improve my grades.

But I hit my lowest slump in my two years there shortly after our return from vacation and was struggling to stay alive in the classroom. My exams were nothing short of dismal and it was Mr. Van Broughton' remarks that were the most disheartening.

I have been disappointed with Billy's work this year, especially this term. He really seems disinterested in school. I am concerned about his overall future especially now, after having seen his SAT scores. I feel that he is really a fine, young, man.

It almost seems as if he has made some decision to dismiss things academic. I do not think, however, that he will respond very well to any more pressure. I continue to respect him highly.

Our SAT tests were administered at Sewanee Military Academy in a room full of Gimps. Most of us were reluctant to even go but there were no other choices available.

"You see that mother fucker in the third row?" Yates asked.

"Yeah," Duck said. "I see him."

"He gave me the finger at the movies last weekend and I don't think I'm going to put up with that shit."

"Why don't we wait until after the tests," Limpy said, trying to intervene.

"There's nothing wrong with right now," Yates interrupted.

He turned in the direction of the cadet and whistled. Everyone else turned in Yates' direction, including the cadet in question. Yates promptly pointed at him and gave him the finger while standing up.

Immediately, there was bedlam. As voices were raised, the room was filled with SMA staff.

"Meet me outside you sonavabitch!" Yates yelled.

Yates was escorted out of the room amid our protests that the cadet had started the whole affair.

The entire morning spent there was a battleground in which the soldiers were assigned a limited and specific space they had to defend but out of which they could not venture. It was as if we had gone to war with strict orders not to fire our weapons.

My performance was dismal. My SAT scores made me eligible for advanced janitorial work at any major university with proper ID and no previous criminal record. As a result, I was prompted to improve my schoolwork.

The six weeks following the disastrous exams, I made honor roll but would never have accomplished that amazing feat had the guidance office not mistakenly averaged Big Sam's mechanical drawing grade in with my other scores. Neither of us said a word and I graciously accepted my certificate and award for my endeavors. It was, indeed, the highlight of my academic winter and I knew from that day forward that if I wanted to, I could do it. I finally realized that I could do it.

There was another event in the making that caused our isolated winter nights to become more bearable. It was a shivering, snowy, Saturday night in early February.

Bobby Larson was a day student although that didn't keep us from being cohorts in a little mischief. He drove to school each day from Cowan, a town on the other side of Monteagle Mountain on the Sewanee side.

On Friday afternoon, when I finished basketball practice, Bobby had just come from wrestling and we were talking privately in the locker room.

"Hey, Billy, want some Jack Daniels tomorrow night?"

"What are you talking about," I asked.

"I'll get you the whiskey and we'll make a drop out on the highway. But the whiskey will cost you ten dollars and the delivery charge is three dollars."

Duck came shuffling by.

"Duck, come here. Bob's got an idea."

Bob started over, all of our heads leaning toward the center of our circle, guarding our words.

"All right, so how do you make the drop?" Duck asked.

"I'll flash my headlights three times as soon as I pass through the Sewanee gates. I'll go down to Deep Woods road, turn around, and somebody will hand you the bottle from the passenger side. You have to be up there near the Sewanee gates. When you see me turning around and you can spot me, have a flashlight with you and cut it on and off three times so we know you're there."

"OK, we're in," Duck whispered. "What time?"

"I'll come through the gates at seven thirty. You be there or I'll kick both your asses on Monday."

"Just don't get caught," I said.

"Don't worry about me," Bob said.

It being so cold, no one, not even the master of the weekend, would be out fanning the bushes. We felt very safe.

When Saturday night arrived, we were hiding next to the highway that ran in front of the school on the side of a hill that sloped steeply down to the edge of the woods next to the Sewanee gates. Droo, Bark, Wreck, Jew-Jew, Hatch and Jody had joined in the adventure.

"It's going to be a hot Saturday night, boys," Duck murmured.

"Yeah, if we don't fucking freeze to death," Hatch said.

"No, it'll be OK. Bob will do fine. Everything's going to be OK," I said assuredly.

When the appointed hour came, we sat shivering in the Cumblerland cold, the icy wind penetrating our winter coats.

"I don't know what the fuck I'm doing out here," Hatch grumbled.

"'Cause you're stupid just like us," Droo moaned.

"Look, there he is," Wreck squeaked, pointing, as Larson drove by heading to Deep Woods road.

Suddenly, we were no longer cold.

"It's him, he's turning around," Hatch affirmed.

"Jody, turn the flashlight on, quick!" I said smiling.

The car began heading toward us, the only one in sight. We were safe. The brown bag was handed out the window from a shadowy, unknown figure. Jody secured the sacred potion as our wayward tribe sprinted through the edge of snowy woods into the black of night.

We made our way clumsily through the woods following the trail of a creek bed that would lead to our hideout. It was no more than a twenty or thirty-minute walk and we were alert as a band of thieves would be, dropping to a squat at the sound of anything threatening.

We assembled in one of the numerous caves down the side of the mountain that was not too far below Piney Point and started a fire. Duck pulled his miner's hat out of a knapsack, lit it, and fastened it to his head.

"I don't know why you wear that stupid thing. You smell like a giant fart," Hatch blared.

"No, Hatch, that's not me, that's the smell of your girlfriend," Duck replied.

"I knew a boy who was wearing one of those," Bark said, "and that shit fell out of his helmet, right on his face, and he was scarred for life, looked like something out of *Tale of Two Cities*, or some shit like that."

"Dipwad, I think you mean *Phantom of the Opera*," Jody argued.

"That's bullshit, Bark," Wreck said, "You don't know anybody like that. I swear, you're the biggest damn liar that—"

"Go to hell, Wreck! I know what the fuck I saw! You—"

"Damnit, shut up!" Duck whispered loudly. "I hear something."

And back to quiet we grew, eyes wide, sipping on illegal whiskey, watching for shadows on the snow.

"It ain't nobody," Jody assured everyone. "We're OK."

We brought cups and bags of food and sat around the fire shooting the bull, sipping our whiskey, and making fun of life and each other. It was a night made for pirates. We lived spectacularly on that lazy, snowy night.

"Man, this is sweet," Jody said, relaxing back onto a boulder.

"Damn sure is. Jew-Jew, don't be a hog. Pass the shiny," Bark said, as the whiskey was passed.

"Well, I know this for sure," Hatch said, "a couple more months and we're out of here. Do you realize we're going to be graduating before too long?"

"Where are you going to college, Hatch?" Jody asked.

"UT. Where else?"

"I got accepted to UA," Jew-Jew replied.

"What's UA?" Duck asked.

"It's only the best university in the whole world . . . the University of Alabama," Jew-Jew replied.

"So, you're a Bama boy . . . I didn't know that," Hatch said.

"Billy, where you going?" Jew-Jew asked.

"I was turned down at Vanderbilt which was no surprise to me but I got accepted at State, so, that's probably where I'll go."

"Which state?" Hatch asked.

"The only state worth attending in the whole world . . . North Carolina State," I said laughing.

"Is that the Tarheels?" Jody asked.

"No, fuckhead," Limpy said, "that's UNC."

"What are you going to major in?" Droo asked.

"I have no idea," I said. "Probably in trying to pass."

"Have any of y'all had to register for the draft?" Hatch asked.

"What are you talking about?" Duck asked.

"The army, dipwad," Hatch replied. "Once you turn eighteen, you have to register for the draft in case there is a war and you get drafted. Have you ever heard of the Vietnam war?"

"Yeah, and I bet some of us end up in that war," Hatch said.

"What does that actually mean?" I asked.

"It means," Hatch replied, "that you have to join the military and that you don't have a choice. You have to join."

"Man, that's bullshit," Wreck squeeked. "Why do you have to do something against your will, I mean, what if you don't want to join?"

"Don't worry, Wreck," Hatch replied, "you're not going to no war because you can't even talk right, so . . ."

"Fuck you," Wreck coughed.

"That's the whole point, Wreck," Droo explained. "It means you don't have a choice."

"Who here has been drafted?" Wreck asked.

"It's not 'drafted'," Hatch explained. "It's called registering for the draft."

"Then, who here's registered for the draft?" Wreck squealed.

Hatch and Bark raised their hands and a pause came between us.

"Billy, you're not eighteen?" Bark asked.

"Nope, not till August. In history, we were talking about what's going on in Vietnam and I sure don't want to fight in that."

The smell of our delicious Jack Daniels whiskey permeated the cave walls as we continued on.

"Shit, don't worry about that," Duck stated. "We won't have to deal with that."

"Where you going to school?" Jody asked Duck.

"I'm going home to Tampa, to the University of South Florida."

"Are you a Gator?" Jew-Jew asked.

"You're from Alabama and you don't know where the Gators go to school? Geez, Jew-Jew, that's the University of Florida, you dipwad," Jody replied.

"What's the difference between Florida and South Florida?" Jew-Jew retorted.

"The people who go to the University of Florida are gators,"

Jody said. "The people who go to the University of South Florida are southern gators."

We laughed and rolled around on the cave floor, warm and safe from the world, from school, and from Vietnam.

Our momentary reprieve was drawing to a close.

"How long have we been here?" Jody asked.

"'Bout three hours," I said.

"Well, I guess, we'd better be getting on back," Hatch said.

"I think you're drunk," Duck said.

"And what if I am?" Hatch said staggering.

"Better figure out a way how not to be drunk in about an hour or they'll cook your ass in hot butter come morning," Bark stated.

When it was time to return, we munched on peppermint candy to camouflage the punishable smell of that sweet whiskey on our breath. We went clear around the back of the school, coming in on Deep Woods road, behind the school store, through the back of St. Dominic's, and over to Hughson Hall. It would take us over an hour to get back but it was worth the precaution.

Everyone arrived back at the dorm safely and inadvertently gathered in the senior lounge to watch television. A serendipitous stroke of spontaneity was guiding our evening.

The rumor was passed that no one had seen Sammy, Weaver, the President or Fuller since supper and that usually meant trouble. Bakerman, a junior, was also missing.

At eleven o'clock, when-lights-out was conducted, they remained on the missing list.

"Where are they?" Duck asked.

"I have no idea. Sammy didn't say anything to me," I explained.

"Well, they better show up quick if they don't want to get in trouble. Speedy's on duty tonight."

"Oh shit," Frankie piped in. "I figure they went into town together, maybe missed their ride, and are walking back."

"No," Jody said, "they'd been back by now,"

We knew the situation was only minutes away from turning into an emergency.

"They better have a good excuse," Robo promised.

I paid no further attention to it and Duck and I fell off to sleep immediately. Around midnight, I was awakened.

"Man," Bakerman said, shaking me awake," you've got to help me!"

"What? What's wrong?" I asked fearfully.

Duck began climbing out of his top bunk.

"Man, we were in the woods having a smoke and a beer when we just sitting there and we heard somebody coming down the road and . . ."

"Were you out in Deep Woods?" Duck asked.

"Yeah, and we were just sitting there and there was these guys in hoods, walking side by side, coming down the road in our direction with flashlights in their hands like the KKK and we just took out of there, everybody started running for their lives! I have no idea where the others are but I guarantee you it ain't good. Something's gone bad wrong down in Deep Woods!"

In seconds, we were dressed and out of the dorm.

As we headed down to Deep Woods, we found Fuller. He took us to the spot where they had been drinking and smoking.

"Fucking-a man, I knew not to do this!" he said, angry with himself.

We called and yelled for the missing seniors but got no reply. We were scared now and didn't know what to do.

We retraced our steps back to campus and went to Speedy's apartment. It was 1:20 A.M. We knocked and then shoved and pushed each other to get out of the way of being the first one Speedy saw when he opened the door. Like an apparition, he was suddenly in our faces and he was mad.

"Speedy, you have to help us," Duck pleaded.

"Boys, about four of you's still missing. What in the world is going on?"

"Bakerman, tell him what happened," Duck said, grabbing Bakerman and dragging him by the collar to the front of the nervous herd.

"Mr. Spangler, I was with some of them when . . ."

"Who's *they*, Mr. Baker?"

"Sammy, Fuller, the Pres . . . I mean Abernathy, Weaver, and me . . . that's all," Baker stated.

"What were you doing out there?" Speedy asked.

Our eyes were riveted on the Fifth Former.

"I was just hanging around with . . ."

"I said what were you doing out there?" Speedy asked forcefully.

"Weaver was getting some water down at the lake for a biology experiment and we just tagged along. We were going to drop back off at the school building and wait while he did some stuff with a microscope or something like that. I was just hanging around with them. That's when we saw the men with hoods."

"The what?" Speedy asked.

"The men in hoods. There were about five or six of them," Baker said.

"Boys, wait for me in front of the dormitory," Speedy said. "We're going to Deep Woods. Dress for the cold."

Our going and coming had created havoc and by this time, other seniors had gathered at their doorways wanting to know what was going on.

By the time we left that dormitory with Speedy at the helm, we were seventeen-strong, all scared out of out wits, thinking we were going to find mutilated carcasses and strewn body parts out on Deep Woods road.

When Speedy would come to a halt to listen to the least of sounds, we would all pile up behind him like a slinky, nobody daring to step out ahead of the man leading this life-threatening expedition to the dark jungles of hooded men and lost boys.

We created more stories on that adventure, more monsters and lizard-skinned beings from hell, everyone having their own gruesome opinion as to what had happened.

My theory was that they had been killed when they accidentally walked up on some moonshiners who were still known to operate in the illegal trade back in the nooks and crannies of Deep Woods Road.

Robo II scared us to death when he stopped, threw his arms out to his side as if to stop everyone from moving, and said, "What's that smell?"

"Billy," Duck whispered to me, "have you got any more peppermint?"

We continued to camouflage our whiskey breath, buried our faces in our winter coats and scarves, and moved on.

We journeyed out beyond the campus grounds and down Deep Woods Road, Speedy knowing every step of the way. In time we came to the spot that was the center of wrongdoing that evening.

"Oh my God, look!" Jody said stunned.

"Is that what I think it is?" Wreck whined.

"Boys," Speedy said, "there's been a crime committed here."

There it sat. Stripped of every recognizable part, everything was gone that could be picked up by hand and carried off. Tires, seats, radio, engine, bumpers. All of it was gone. Seems the only piece of Father Hazelton's car that was left was the front license plate that read, "Peace."

"Boys, this was a car theft gang out of Chattanooga. I've seen this before. I hope the missing boys didn't run into them. If they did, there's trouble. Let's double back to school right now."

We broke off in a jog with about two miles to go.

"Speedy didn't mean trouble, he meant homicide," Bakerman said breathing heavily.

"If they'd killed them, they'd killed them and put them in the car, like trophies or something," Robo I argued.

"What the fuck are you talking about, you idiot?" Duck said. "Nobody's dead. They're all right, I know they are."

Our frozen breath shot from our nostrils, the flashlights portraying a herd of horses moving swiftly through the Deep Woods forest.

Sammy, Fuller, Weaver and the President were waiting on the steps of Hughson Hall when we returned.

When Speedy saw them, he walked right past them to the administration building. Without being asked, they knew what to do and followed sheepishly behind him.

"Bakerman, anybody been drinking?" Bullet asked.

"All of them," he replied.

The next morning, there we sat in Sammy's room, listening to the tale that lasted the rest of the year, the imminent death of five scoundrels scurrying around in the bushes for a drink and a smoke.

It was heartwarming and uplifting to hear, to see the eyes aglow, the adrenalin pumping in our veins, and the exaggeration of every step taking each of us to higher spaces. It made the hair on the back of your neck bristle.

If that story was told once, it was told a dozen times, each delivery changing bit by bit the original event. By the time we hit the sack the following night, you would have thought that it was a military skirmish that took place in our own backyard.

Our stories were the sources of our earned mythologies, origins of inspiration passed down for years to come. All of us had escaped the past night of recklessness and all felt blessed for it. None of us would attempt to scale the fence again. It was time to focus on the finish line.

Winter was forgotten momentarily and we went about our business the next day, offering our condolences to Father Hazelton who was discouraged by a continued avalanche of reminders of his misfortune. The spell of winter's seductive melancholy was over.

CHAPTER 18

Father Hazelton and the Battle of Caen

We marched into the last three months of school with the anticipation of baseball and graduation on our minds.

During this entire period of time from January until April, there were few, if any, letters written home. I neither had the time nor the desire to do so. Mother's communications picked up around the end of March partly because of the upcoming graduation and partly because of the need to make decisions about college.

She was adamant about the cause of my erroneous misfortune of feeling unmotivated about attending North Carolina State and made clear over spring break what she felt was the source . . . my preoccupation with my depression. I wrote to her in the latter part of March, shortly after our return from spring vacation.

Mom,

I got your letter today and there are a few things I'd like to say. I completely understand what you mean by having moods that dominates one's life and causes you to reject and neglect your friends and family. I said that I understood that in your letters. However, over the phone I could not understand what you were trying to say nor could I understand at home. I don't mind being criticized but I don't care to be yelled at time after time after time again.

If you would take the time to explain to me while I'm at home, as you do in your letters, I would be perfectly content and could easily understand your feelings. However, there is only one way I have found to escape when everyone is down on you and that is to run and try and figure it out yourself. I am alone with my problems and I find that at times it is hard.

There are times when a person can be all mixed up and he sees no way out, so he tries to back up his feelings by trying to talk his way out. I tried and I was wrong. According to you, most of the things I've done in the past have been wrong.

When times get bad and nobody will take time to talk to me and try and understand me, then, I always run from it. It seems I always have.

If you and if only you want things to work out they can. It is entirely up to you. I will join in. I have tried and it didn't work. I don't ask for anything. Just understanding. But I'm tired of always being wrong.

Probably what I've said is wrong as usual and you are mad. Mad because I'm trying to say what I think is right instead of what is right. Do I really know the difference?

Apparently, the other times I didn't. You said nothing wrong in your letter simply because when I opened it, I had an open mind and it didn't yell at me.

Love,
Billy

As winter rolled into a thawing spring on the mountain, baseball submerged all of my problems out of sight and I gave my attention to nothing else. The Varsity Club redesigned the guidelines of initiation and there would be no more hazing. Lizard had left an indelible mark on the school with the prank the year before and this year's crew was treated with respect and honor for their athletic accomplishments. No one dared repeat the crime.

Instead of wearing vegetables around their necks and reptiles in their underwear, the new initiates wore suits and ties and an embroidered band around their sleeves denoting their upcoming membership. Times were changing.

As spring continued to warm, I, too, changed my mind about college and wanted to stay at St. Andrew's another year. I considered deliberately failing history that would keep me from graduating and there would be no choice. I thought that if I could stay here, take several advanced courses in science and math, I would be better prepared.

I shared this bonehead idea with no one and completed a pitiful term paper in history on the horrors of the Andersonville concentration camp and never even had the paper returned to me. The term paper was a horror unto itself. I would give Mr. Van Broughton the benefit of the doubt and assume that my paper was not worth returning.

In any case, April and May came on quickly and before I knew it, graduation was only a month away. I didn't need a calendar to keep up with the passing of time or the seasons. I always knew when I had been confined to the campus for too long because of a weekly event that took place in the chapel. It was a dead giveaway.

"C'mon Billy, let's go! Hustle up! We've got to get on the end of the pew," Duck yelled.

Chapel was minutes away. We hurried past the midget-sized underformers handing out church bulletins.

"I know it, man, both of them are going to walk right by us and I bet she's wearing that white panty hose today."

"She wore stockings last Sunday," I whispered.

And there we sat, waiting for the angels to take communion. Lisa and Mary Alice, the daughters of Father Chamberlain, were the first girls ever at St. Andrew's.

Both girls were attractive to all of us, but when confined to campus too long, they each took on an absolutely gorgeous, seductive air about themselves. Their seductiveness signaled as well that it was time to go home.

"Flat Tire just told me they're not here today," I whispered.

"How does he know?" Duck asked.

"He said Father C's out of town and took the girls with him," I explained.

"Fucking-a," Duck moaned, "that figures."

We sat and sang the hymns, strolled up to the altar to take communion, all the while our thoughts lost in the lustful imaginings of the absent angels. That night, restless, I walked down to the lake during study hall.

The moon was just above the horizon as the still cool spring nights whistled through the tree limbs and lakeside brush. The water was motionless, a perfect May mirror.

As I rose to head back to the dormitory, I saw a figure walking toward me. It was Father Hazelton.

"Good evening, Billy," he said as he approached.

"Hello, Father," I replied.

"You probably ought to head back to your dormitory. You're not supposed to be down here."

"Yes, sir," I said. "I was just doing some thinking."

"Thinking about what?" he asked, as he turned and joined me in my walk around the gymnasium and toward St. Joseph's.

"Before you begin, let me make a suggestion. How about some hot chocolate in my apartment and we'll talk some there?" he asked.

"Sure," I said, "I'm caught up in my work."

I said hello to his wife upon entering and followed him into his study. The children were on their way to bed.

"Make yourself at home," he said pointing to the sofa.

I leaned back, perfectly at ease in his presence, and joined my hands behind my head.

"So, how are you, Billy?"

"I'm fine," I said. "I'm a little anxious about graduation. I mean, part of me doesn't really want to leave."

"That's a far cry from last October, isn't it?" he asked.

"Yes, sir, it is. That was pretty dumb on my part. I just didn't know any better. I probably should have talked to you about it before I did it but once I started selling my stuff, it seemed like there was no turning back and it was too late."

"As you can see, it turned out fine. By the way, I heard you were accepted at North Carolina State."

"Yes, sir, I was. I was turned down at two others."

"But you were accepted at one. Sometimes, all we need is one chance. Are you going to go there?"

"I guess so. I'm not sure what I want to do," I explained. "It's pretty confusing to me. And I realize part of me is afraid."

"Why?" he asked.

"I don't know. I worry about whether or not I can make it academically. But I've thought about trying out for baseball."

"My bet would be that you would do well at both. You're not a quitter, Billy. You know how to hang in there and work it out."

"It seems that sometimes I've had no choice. I have a friend that goes to a private school in New Hampshire and he says the reason he's survived the school he's at is because he wakes up everyday and finds out he isn't dead, so, there's nothing else to do but go ahead and do what you're supposed to do."

"Is that how you feel?" he asked.

"Sometimes," I said.

Mrs. Hazelton brought in the hot chocolate and a plate of chocolate chip cookies. She smiled and turned to leave.

"Dear, would you mind closing the door?" he asked.

"Thank you," I said, reaching for several cookies.

"Tell me about your family and how they are doing. How does your mother feel about you attending State?" he asked.

"I'm sure she's happy about it. She has always worried that I would never go to college. She has always worried about my grades."

"And does your father know? Do you have any contact with him? I know your mother and father were divorced."

"No, sir, I don't think he does. I think he lives out in California somewhere. My mother and father were divorced when Sammy and I were two. But I don't remember him and have never seen him. I wouldn't have any idea as how to get in touch with him."

"Do you want to?" he asked.

"Yes, I think so. He's my father no matter what happened. I would like to know where I came from . . . I guess."

"Hold on one minute, I have to go to the kitchen for a second," he said.

He returned in a few moments.

"You had a stepfather, didn't you?"

Immediately, I was seized with the urge to leave. I do not want to go here, I said to myself.

"Yes, sir, I did. My mother married him when I was seven. He died in an industrial accident when I was fourteen."

"Did you get along with him?" Father Hazelton asked.

"No, sir, I did not," I said. "I remember I cried at the funeral but I didn't like him and I didn't want him to be around him any more. So, when he died, it was a paradox for me. I was glad he was gone and at the same time, was sad that he died."

"Did you have a good relationship with him?"

I fumbled around and paused. Like it or not, it was time to choose.

"No, sir, I did not. He was mean and out of control a lot of the time. He would hit you for no reason at all. When he came home from work, I would usually go outside and stay there until I had to come home for supper."

"When did you get your schoolwork done?"

"Sometimes I wouldn't. It was too scary being in the house in case he got mad at you for something. I remember one time he was building a carport onto the house and there was an opening that led into the attic. So, being the way I am, I climbed up there one day, climbed inside the house and started exploring. I didn't get very far because I stepped off of the rafters onto the soft stuff and fell through the bathroom ceiling. I almost killed myself. The whole ceiling in the bathroom was destroyed and I knew he was going to be coming home in about an hour. So, I didn't know what to do. I couldn't fix it, I didn't know how. So, I waited. And when he drove in the driveway, I walked out, met him, and told him what happened. I bet I cried for two days after he beat the hell out of me . . . sorry Father, after he beat me so hard for so long."

"What did your mother do?" Father Hazelton asked.

"Nothing."

"Did she love your stepfather?" he asked.

I paused again.

"I don't know how she could have. I saw him hit her one time and knock her to the floor. I was at the end of the hall and she saw me. She was on the floor when she saw me and she stretched out on the floor and closed the door. I wanted to help but I couldn't. I knew he would kill me."

"Did your mother know how you felt?"

I gained as much balance as I could.

"I don't know. How could she not know that he was mean?" I asked.

Father Hazelton did not reply but waited patiently, giving me the time I needed to reply. I began to feel the surge in my chest working its way up my throat and I was powerless to hold it back. I did everything I could to stop it, short of just getting up and walking out of the room.

"He had no right to do to me what he did," I mumbled. I began to slowly crumble.

He pulled his chair directly in front of me, his arm on my shoulder. "Tell me Billy, tell me what happened if you want to," he said.

"I don't even remember when it started, it seems so long ago but no matter what I do, I can't make it go away. I can't forget what he did," I said. I was falling apart, dissolving completely.

"It's OK. You're going to make it through this. Don't stop."

"He would come into our bedroom late at night. I guess sometimes it was early in the morning and he would get in bed with one of us. Sometimes he would get in bed with Sammy, sometimes me," I said straining. "I don't think I can do this, I don't think I can tell you," I said without conviction.

"It's OK, Billy. You're going to make it through. It's your choice. You've been dealing with this for so long. It's time to get this monkey off your back. You will make it through."

I picked back up, wiping the snot and tears from my face.

"He would come in our room and get in our bed and start touching us and he would make me touch him and I just wanted to die," I said, my voice breaking up, my sobbing taking over.

"What would Sammy be doing when this took place?" he asked.

"Nothing. Nobody could do anything. Sammy did the same thing I did. I turned my back to them so I couldn't see. It didn't help because you still saw it in your mind and there was no way out," I said.

"Do you and Sammy talk about this between the two of you?"

"No, Sam won't talk about it. He says my problem is I'm too sensitive and I take things personally. I think he won't talk about it because he's scared. He just wants to pretend it never happened. He just wants to pretend it doesn't exist. God, I wish I could be like him," I said crying.

"Tell me more. It's OK to keep talking. Don't stop now. We will work our way through this," Father Hazelton said.

"He would make you put your mouth . . . oh God, I can't do this," I said, as I doubled over, my intestines cramping, my face feeling distorted, my whole body under siege.

"Don't give up, don't go back inside. Keep telling me about it," he said, more forcefully than before. "You're going to make it through this, I promise."

As I raised my head from my knees, my blurred vision saw him only inches from me and I felt his strong arm on my shoulder. It was all I needed. It was all I ever wanted.

"He would make me put my mouth on him and I just wanted to die. I knew this wasn't right and the worst thing about it was I couldn't defend myself. I couldn't protect myself from him!" I screamed. "I know Mother knew. I know she knew what he was doing to us! She had to know that he wasn't in her bed with her so, where was he? He was in the bed with us and nobody could do anything about it!" I yelled.

As the volcano erupted, time ceased to exist.

"Did you ever tell your mother?"

"No," I said taking a breath. "What was there to tell? I felt like she knew what was going on and she didn't do anything about it. She didn't protect me from him but I don't think she could have. She was just like us . . . trapped," I cried as I collapsed into the arms of one of the only men I trusted. And at that moment, I died.

Father Hazelton began holding me, whispering into my ear over and over.

"Everything is fine now. Everything is going to work out. Everything is fine now. Everything is going to work out."

My skin was burning hot snot and tears unleashed into the open from the abyss in which they had been hidden for years.

I became a little boy all over again, clamping tightly to the man in front of me who offered me a baptism of truth, of release, and of beginning the process of facing my enemy.

As the tears and upset moved through the wall of repressed grief and anger, the moment softened into the twilight of greater understanding.

"I apologize for cussing. I'm still so angry about it," I said.

"It's certainly OK. I understand. You have a right to be. Anyone would be."

"A couple of months before he died, I had decided to take care of it. I wanted to kill him. I took a chair and stood beside the front door to see where I had to stand on it when he came through the door to swing a baseball bat and hit him square on the head. Part of me had decided to do that if nothing changed. I hated him so much."

"He beat you to the punch, Billy," Father Hazelton said. "It was time for him to go."

We talked for another hour, the lateness now beyond recovery for the next day for either one of us.

"What do I do now? Do I tell my mother, do I talk to her about it?" I asked.

"There is going to be plenty of time to do that. You've learned tonight that you don't have to keep this inside of you, that you can talk about your problems with people who love you, who care for you. There will be many more opportunities to address this even after you leave St. Andrew's. In the meantime, there is work to do. You have to focus on graduation and getting your schoolwork done and not finding yourself lounging at the lake when you need to be in your room."

"I am sorry about that," I said. "I'll get focused and I won't be off where I'm not supposed to be."

"But think of it. Had you not been at the lake, we might not have had the chance to talk. Funny how things usually work out."

"Yes," I said, "I'm happy you came along. Thank you. I've never told anybody about this. I'm too ashamed."

"Billy, do you know how much Speedy and Father Henry and Mr. Jordan and Mr. Gautier . . . do you know how much they think of you, how proud all of us are of you?" he asked.

"I try hard most of the time. Most of the time, I try to do my best."

"Billy, you didn't answer my question."

"Do I know?" I asked. I paused with a now even, deep breath. "I guess so," I said.

"No, you don't. You think you're less than that because of what has happened to you, because of what was not your choice. But look at what you have accomplished here in two years!" he said laughing. "And yet, the past is always gone and we have to start over. We have to begin anew each day of our lives to live out the purpose we have chosen."

"I don't know what that purpose is, Father," I said beginning to cry again.

"You will, Billy, you will one day know . . . *if,*" he said pointing at me, "*if* it is your desire to know. If it's your choice."

With those words, with both of us exhausted, we fell silent for a moment.

"Let me see if I can explain something to you," he said. "When something happens to us, it becomes part of our experience. When we experience something, it is lodged in our minds and it is not going to go away. It's not going to go away because it's in our experience. Do you understand so far?"

"Yes, sir, I do," I said.

"It's like using a tape recorder. Once you record it, it's on the tape. It's not going anywhere. Now your mind is very similar. Your experiences with your stepfather are lodged in your mind. They are recorded in your mind, as it were. The question is how you are going to choose to respond to that tape. Again . . . and I'm not trying to avoid discussing the issue . . . it is your choice. And that may take you a very long time in your mind to decide."

"I understand," I said wiping my tears. "Sometimes I just get overwhelmed with it and don't know what to do."

"That is the plight of the majority of people. But Billy, you're learning. You've decided to talk about it. You've decided to be courageous enough to bring it out in the open instead of harboring it inside of yourself for the rest of your life. What you deny, what you fight against in your mind will always grow stronger. Stop resisting and know that what you have done tonight is part of how you will come to terms with your stepfather. Resistance is suffering."

"I'm so tired of fighting this," I said, my head bowed, buried in my hands.

He gently placed his right hand around the back of my head and squeezed lightly. "You are going to make it. You are going to make it," he whispered. "You are strong and you're going to make it."

I looked in his eyes for just a moment, put my arms around him, hugged him, and said, "Thank you for listening to me. Thank you for everything you've done for me. I don't think I could have made it without you."

I could go no further.

"You are quite welcome, Billy. It's the reason I am here. C'mon and I'll walk you back to your room. I'm sure they're wondering where you are. By the way, when I went to the kitchen, I called Father Henry. He knows you've been with me."

"OK," I said. "I sure don't want to get another paddling anytime soon."

When I returned to my room, Duck was fast asleep. I crawled unnoticed into bed, feeling lighter and stronger. I looked at the clock. It was 1:45.

That night, the nightmare returned.

Hiding childishly in the closet, I begin to suffocate under the weight of my own terror. I hear the cocking sound of the German Luger pistol and know that it is leveled head-high, awaiting my decision as to the moment of my execution. I am moments from my death.

This time, as the end of the dream draws close and the air is quickly leaving the closet in which I am incarcerated, I make a different decision.

"If I am going to die," I say to myself, "then I am going to die facing my enemy."

I stand up straight, take a deep breath, and swing the door open, turning my head to the left to find myself looking slightly over the eyesight and barrel of the German Luger pistol.

As my eyes swiftly begin the search past the barrel for the eyes of my killer, to let him know that before I died that I am going to die courageously, I realize that the German soldiers are gone and that the gun is held by not a German solider but a man I know. It is my stepfather.

Our eyes lock. Within seconds of recognizing the executioner and his recognition of me, the scene evaporates and I find myself by a stream near the cottage, splashing water over my head and face. My heart is racing.

Instinctively, I know I have survived the skirmish and know the war is coming to an end. Tired but peaceful, I give thanks for another day. Only a while longer, I think. It's only a short while longer. I am going to make it.

I suddenly awoke and looked at the clock once more. It was 4:35. I rose, walked to the window and peered outside, leaning on the cold, metal frame of the window.

I walked sleepily to the bathroom down the hall where I urinated and drank a glass of water. I returned to my bed without the full understanding of what had just happened. It would be the last time the nightmare would haunt me.

I closed the window and climbed in bed thinking of Father Hazelton and his kindness and love. In the silence and darkness of that night, I fell back to sleep in the shelter and sanctuary of St. Andrew's School and the anticipation of meeting the Gimps for the last time on the baseball field in three days.

CHAPTER 19

Speedy's Revenge

We raced to the chapel to ring the bell. Twenty-seven times we rang it. It was a new school record for the most runs scored in a game.

"God, Yates," I said, "that's about the longest ball I have ever seen hit. Jesus, you killed it!" I said.

"I swear, as soon as it left his hand, I knew it was my pitch. Jesus, what an a-hole. It was perfect! I NNOKIed that thing" Yates yelled.

"Is anybody counting? Was that seventeen or eighteen?" Big Sam yelled.

"I'm counting . . . you got two more . . . quick!" Make screamed.

Three or four others grabbed the rope and yanked down for two more rings. A pause of fifteen seconds separated the winners from the loser as we then rang out three runs for the losers, their bus turning onto the main road to head home empty-handed.

We walked up to the quad, our cleats scrapping the asphalt.

"Sammy, look," Bakerman said, pointing to his right foot, "there's blood on your shoe."

The fifth former felt proud to be walking with us. He would take his place as a senior and a prefect among this elite group in a short while.

"Damn right," Big Sam said. "You remember that slide at second?"

We all acknowledged the memory with gusto.

"Well, I thought I took his wrist off! Stupid a-hole thought he was going to get me. I swear, my cleat went straight up his arm."

"Gimp blood," Bakerman said, "sweet as wine."

"What the fuck do you know about wine, you little twit?" Weaver argued.

And we were off again in our own world, a world inhabited only by the selected, initiated royalty. We were kings of this mountain top if but for the day.

I savored that final day of baseball throughout the night and the final weeks to come. It was what mattered most to me. To be on the mound, to lead the charge, this was my kingdom, my favorite place in the world. On Monday, we were back to class with only two weeks to go.

"Billy, wait up," Duck said. "Look what I found in Dimwitt's room."

He reached in his pocket, cupped the obviously illegal item in his palm, and showed me the M-80 cherry bomb.

"Did you tell him you took it?" I asked.

"Hell, no," he said, "why would I do that?"

We paused. "What do you want to do with it?" he asked.

"I know exactly what to do with it," I said. "But if we get caught, there ain't no way we can dig a hole deep enough to escape. If we're anywhere near it when it goes off, we're dead."

The next morning at break, we worked on a time fuse with a cigarette and had it down to about ninety seconds before the explosion would take place. We planted it right outside Hughson Hall, behind the bushes, set to go off in the middle of break when the student traffic would be the heaviest.

Everything went as planned and no sooner did we hit the entrance to the school building than the bomb exploded, sending echoes across the entire campus. The noise penetrated the entrance way so heavily that several people ducked, thinking that something had exploded near them. I was waiting for flying glass and body parts to splatter against the brick front. Instantly, I knew I had made a tremendous mistake. But it was too late.

I sat in class alone, praying. As the class filled up fifteen minutes later, all anyone could talk about was the bomb, who was responsible, and what the punishment would be.

Mr. Sherwin returned to start class and asked if anyone knew anything about it. Nobody answered and he began listing algebra problems on the blackboard for the day. No sooner had he started, than Father Henry appeared at the door.

"Mr. Sherwin, may I see Mr. McNeal?"

"Jesus Christ," I thought to myself, "God must have told him." There was no other way he could have found out so quickly.

"Mr. McNeal, I'd like for you to put your dormitory on bounds until we find the culprit who set off that bomb. Mr. Gautier' five year old son was walking by when the (Oh Jesus, I killed a child . . .) bomb went off and (Shit, I know it, I know it . . . it blew his foot off . . .) it scared him so badly that he is still crying. I can't believe that (Oh Father, I can't either, I don't know why I did such a dumb thing, I'm so goddamn stupid . . .) someone would do such a ridiculous thing. But your dormitory will remain on bounds until we catch him."

I steadied my legs and spoke.

"Father, I've already caught him."

"You know who it is, Mr. McNeal?" he replied, pleasantly surprised to find out so soon.

"Yes, sir." I looked in his eyes quivering.

"Who was the scoundrel, Mr. McNeal?"

I did not hesitate. "Well, Father, it was me."

I bowed my head.

"You, Mr. McNeal. Of all people, you?"

"Yes, sir."

"Mr. McNeal, I will speak to you later."

He turned around and walked out of the school building without any further discussion. I returned to class with legs of putty and fear the size of a bowling ball in the pit of my stomach. I knew that my honesty this time would do me no good.

At lunchtime my name was called. I received a round of applause that added little to my demise.

I walked into Speedy's office. He was sitting there grinning. It was a tremendous privilege for him and I was some prize for him. President of the class, president of the Varsity Club, prefect.

"Please, Speedy, don't paddle me. I'll do anything, I'll . . ."

"Oh you're going to get it this time, Mr. Mac!" he said laughing, his right hand firmly grasped around the paddle, slapping the palm of his left. He was enjoying the moment.

"The punishment is going to be three licks in front the entire dormitory. We'll get this over with right after supper tonight."

"Speedy, please, anything but licks," I pleaded vainly.

My attempts at negotiating fell on deaf ears.

That evening, that dreaded evening, everyone in my dormitory raced back from supper to line up in the hall where they could get a good view of my execution.

"Man, this is going to be a real de-assination," a little fifth former said as I stepped out into the hall to meet my maker.

In preparation for the show, Duck and I worked out a plan to help me deal with Speedy's paddle. If Speedy came up with a half-swing, Duck was to blink his eyes once. I would know under those conditions that it would not be life threatening.

If it was a full swing, Duck was to blink his eyes twice. Then, I would know that all hell was about to break loose and stiffen for the worst.

As I stepped out into the hall, they were all there, Speedy slapping the paddle every two or three seconds in his left hand, just smiling at me.

"Let's go, Mr. Mac and get this over with."

I was not trembling but knew this was what I deserved. I approached willingly.

Each of the underclassmen huddled there to prod Speedy on with pleas for dismemberment. But Duck threatened them and they became quiet.

I positioned myself, bending only slightly over. Duck was in front of me, ready to help.

"OK. Here we go," Speedy said.

I looked up at Duck. One blink. Whack. Oh Jesus, my ass is on fire. I can't take any more.

I looked up again. One blink. Whack. It knocked the air right out of my mouth and I stumbled forward.

"One more, Mr. Mac," Speedy said quietly.

I looked up to find Duck covering both of his eyes. Wham!

He lifted me off the tile floor and my rear went numb. I could feel it pulsating against my sweatpants, swollen and hot as the tears leaped from my eyes. Without saying a word but taking my punishment in stride, I retreated to my room, followed by Speedy and Duck, echoes of retreating footsteps in the hall.

When the two of them came in, I lay on my stomach with my face down in the pillow.

"Mr. Mac, I hated doing that to you." And I knew he did. "But that was a pretty lame stunt you pulled. Get up here right now," he said.

I stood up, my hands wiping away my tears.

As he was hugging me, he said, "You'll be missed around here next year. Billy, you're a fine young man. Don't let this get you down. You created this yourself. You made a bad choice."

"Now I know why they call you Speedy," I said as humorously as I could. He smiled, patted me on the back and walked out.

"That man is fast, isn't he?" Duck said.

"Fucking-a," I said returning to my bed.

I apologized to Mr. and Mrs. Gautier and was quickly forgiven. It was over with in one day with a lot of congratulations for my prank coming from my friends and other younger boys.

I felt fine and spoke warmly with Speedy only an hour after supper the next night. All in all, I would have to say that it was worth it. I returned to the fold with a medal of valor on my chest.

Graduation was around the corner.

CHAPTER 20

Exiting the Cocoon

As the end of May approached, we were in a daze, excited and impatient, yet, we silenced our feelings of regret about leaving. Nostalgia was the fiber of conversation and every second of time spent at St. Andrew's over the last two years was relived and reinvented. When we couldn't remember the facts, we simply substituted our own realities.

It was a thunderous time of the year with rebel yells and celebration. I looked around me and saw boys I knew I would never see again in my life, boys who had become family to me, brothers in the truest sense of the word whose clothes I wore and whose food I shared. A massive den of thirty-two baby wolves groomed to split off and hunt on their own gathered boisterously before stampeding off for the first time alone and the last time together.

There was a huge hole in my heart where each one resided and even though it may have been difficult to express, it was felt and acknowledged in our tribe without ever saying a word. The bond was stitched tightly and was revered by each of us as we waited for the grand weekend to begin. In my time at St. Andrew's, I had learned a great deal about many things but I had never been taught how to say goodbye.

This was forty-eight hours of excruciating but necessary farewells, a spectacular weekend spanning one long goodbye. As I was sitting at my desk two days before Mother's arrival, I vainly attempted to scribble out the words that were spoken from my heart.

To Father Henry . . . thank you for your confidence in me and for giving me the chance to prove myself, in spite of the dumb bomb thing. I can't and never will be able to thank you enough.

To Father Hazelton . . . thank you for being there when I needed you, for your encouragement and love when I didn't think I could go on. I will never be able to tell you what you mean to me.

To Mr. Gautier . . . thank you for caring so much about me, and helping me learn to think. I don't think I've ever learned as much in a class before. I will never forget you.

To Speedy . . . thank you for saying what you did after you paddled me. I trust you and know you did what you had to do. Thanks for always smiling and making St. Andrew's what it is.

To Granny . . . thank you for being so kind and so nice to me. You're like a mother and I will always remember the story about you and Herman getting caught running moonshine to Nashville. Granny, I'll miss you so much.

To Mrs. Foster . . . thanks for always giving me extra food when I was hungry and checking on me. You're like family to me and it's hard leaving, thinking I won't see you again.

To Mr. Jordan . . . thanks for being so different and thinking that I'm good in English. I want you to know how much I respect you and admire you.

To Mr. Sherwin and Mr. Van Broughton . . . I apologize for being so dumb and wish that I could have made your job easier.

To Mrs. Tate . . . you were always a friend to me and I can't think of St. Andrew's without thinking of you and your family. I hope that you'll still be here when I come back to visit. Thanks for letting me charge food to my account.

To everyone else, I leave knowing that I did the best I could do even though at times that wasn't very remarkable. I don't want to leave St. Andrew's but know that I must.

"You're not actually going to give them the satisfaction, are you?" the President asked when he peered over my shoulder and saw my letter.

"I thought I might," I said.

"Never let them know what you're thinking," he said smiling.

"Yes, that strategy worked out pretty well for you, didn't it?" I said.

We both laughed and arms around one another's shoulders, we headed to the quad.

Mother arrived with Aunt Evelyn and Uncle Charlie early Friday afternoon. We all went out to eat with several other families and it was a proud moment for everybody. Just making it through St. Andrew's seemed to be enough for a lot of boys and their parents.

Graduation morning, the chapel was packed an hour before mass began, everyone hoping to get a respectable seat. We were seated on the right, on the aisle side, about ten pews from the front, pressed tightly against one another to make room for other people.

I scanned every speck of chipped paint, every screw of every light fixture, every face of every friend to whom I was saying goodbye. I read the graffiti on every hymnal and prayer book in front of me and when I had the chance, I wrote, "I just signed this hymnal and can't nobody do anything about it because I just graduated. McNeal I /1969."

It was a long wait for our turn to walk and kneel for the last time at the altar. When I finally did make my way to the first step, I surrendered to my leaving and prayed more fervently than ever before.

Father Henry walked slowly down the rail, placing the wafer in each person's hand, repeating quietly, "Take, eat, this is my body which was broken for you. Eat this in remembrance of me."

As my turn for a sip of wine came and I placed my lips on the rim of the silver chalice, the sweet taste of the sherry caused my lips to pucker slightly. As I raised my head, I saw him eye to eye again, his smile dangling over my head like a halo. I felt holy and blessed.

When the awards ceremonies came, it was a mesmerizing event with an abundance of priests and monks in robes, pomp and gifts of frankincense and myrrh. Father Deter, the Prior, looked strikingly more like Christ than ever before in his High Mass attire and drew silence as he moved about. The heavy incense caused little children to cover their mouths and gag loudly, drawing attention to themselves only momentarily.

Father Deter began with words of welcome and priestly parable, while the Czar was going over his notes, smiling, his beak glowing red with anticipation and warmth. When Father Henry took the podium, I fixed my eyes on this great man and studied him, thinking it would be for the last time.

As best I could at the age of seventeen, I allowed to form in my mind, an ever-growing and expanding understanding of just how much he had done for me and what his life had meant to me. Are there other men such as he that reside in communities, in homes, in the workplace who willingly take a young boy under his wings and transfer as best he can, his knowledge of becoming a man to him?

I knew none before coming to St. Andrew's. There was nothing more than a complete absence of what I have come to know as men in my life up to that time and Father Henry and the others were able to fill some of that void.

In my first year at St. Andrew's, I saw him first-hand only on those occasions that were potentially punishable for me but I saw him walk, breathe, listen, and lead from a distance and those were valuable times as well. He did not have to be with me every second to feed me, to allow me to share in what he wished for every boy.

In my second year, being with him everyday for an hour was the equivalent of being allowed to visit the king and hear his stories. As you were led back to the everyday routine, you could direct yourself from the point of view gained in his presence, in the midst of the simplest of chores. But youth is a horrible time to learn to be grateful for what is helping your world continue to orbit and it is frequently taken for granted, settling instead for an amnesic existence, entranced with mediocrity and failure of sight.

I could not say which of those two years meant more, one absent from him, one in his presence. They were both rewarding and he taught me even when he did not know I was there. As I watched him that day, I realized that I did love him and that I was indebted to him, not being the least bit cognizant of what he had really done for me. I was equally unaware of the years it would take to manifest those lessons in my life.

The athletic awards began taking place. Coach Winton rose to take the podium.

"This has really been a wonderful year not only for the team but for myself personally. I want to acknowledge the superb performance of several players . . . Sam McNeal, McNeal II, perhaps one of the finest catchers we've had in a long time . . . stand up, Sam. Sam was MVP last year."

Sam rose and we applauded.

"In our record setting game against the Academy this year, Sam hit two triples, a home run, and a double. I might also add that if you're ever playing second or third base and you see Sam McNeal sliding to your base, I want to suggest that you get out of the way as soon as you can."

We erupted in laughter.

"Sam, you'll be missed."

"Ben Yates who threw a no-hitter against Castle Heights Military, Ben, stand up."

Ben rose and there was a standing ovation. "Ben's fastball is perhaps unhittable. He can play college ball if he chooses to. Ben, thank you for all of your hard work."

"An underclassman joined our ranks this year and proved to be a valuable asset to the team. Lynn Egerton. Lynn, please stand."

Lynn was shy but would be the starting pitcher in the new season ahead. He wiggled his hand to acknowledge Coach Winton's accolades.

"Before I name the most valuable player, I want to tell a story about this young man. He was pitching against Huntland and we were ahead by two runs. He gave up two singles and was faced with having to make some decisions. I gave his brother, who was catching, a signal for a fastball but he shook it off. His brother gave him the signal again but he shook it off again. If you know these two boys, you know they can fuss. So, Sam gave him the signal again but this time, he was so mad, he stood and stuck his finger out in front of the plate. His brother shook it off again and before I knew it, they almost had a knock-down drag-out right there halfway between home plate and the mound. I ran out on the field, took both of them by the collar, and pulled them right up to my face. I said, 'What did he tell you to throw?' His brother said, 'A fastball.'" And I said, 'Then, throw it.' He looked at me and said, 'Yes, sir, but he can hit my fast ball . . . he can't hit my curve.' 'How do you know?' I asked him. And he said, 'Trust me. He can't hit my curve.' So, I said, throw the curve. He struck him out on the curveball. And once the boys settled down, we got 'em out and won the game."

He shifted his weight and began again.

"I remember this boy when he first came to St. A. I used to watch him go down to the lake all of the time and sulk. I knew he was homesick and he was eaten up with it. I wondered if he was going to make it. But he eventually got over that and became a good ball player. I'm proud to say that the most valuable player goes to Billy McNeal, pitcher and third baseman."

As I rose and made my way out of the row, Sam patted me on the back. "You deserve it," he said.

Duck jumped up and hugged me.

As I shook Coach Winton's hand, I said, "Thank you so much. I really do appreciate this."

"Billy, you deserve this. You'll be missed."

There were smaller acknowledgements accorded to the prefects for their hard work in the dormitory and the student council but that was just part of the territory and reaped no substantial gains for any of us. Nonetheless, there was a sort of mystic and magic that fueled the show.

The diplomas were handed out in spectacular fashion, with ample time for all attention to be riveted on each boy as he walked sheepishly alone to receive two handshakes and a maroon-covered folder with his diploma inside. One by one, grinning, teeth shining, we walked. It was soon time for Father Hazelton to speak.

"Father Facetious! Father Facetious!" we whispered respectfully.

He turned to us with a sincere, warm, smile and said, "Thank you, boys, for that introduction."

It did not bother him in the least and he could see our love for him. Then, he planted his feet to speak.

He opened with a poem from the posthumous writings of the Magister Ludi, Joseph Knecht, a Herman Hesse character in the novel, *The Glass Bead Game*. I had read it many times from the books I borrowed from Mr. Gautier.

> As every flower fades and as all youth
> Departs, so life at every stage,
> So every virtue, so our grasp of truth,
> Blooms in its day and may not last forever.
> Since life may summon us at every age
> Be ready, heart, for parting, new endeavor,
> Be ready bravely and without remorse
> To find new light that old ties cannot give.
> In all beginnings dwells a magic force
> For guarding us and helping us to live.
>
> Serenely let us move to distant places
> And let no sentiments of home detain us.
> The Cosmic Spirit seeks not to restrain us
> But lifts us up stage by stage to wider spaces.
> If we accept a home of our own making,
> Familiar habit makes for indolence.
> We must prepare for parting and leave-taking
> Or else remain the slaves of permanence.
>
> Even the hour of our death may send
> Us speeding on to fresh and newer spaces,
> And life may summon us to newer races.
> So be it, heart: farewell without end.

The power of his words and the intonation of his voice rendered me breathless, so in awe of this experience that I did not want to leave. It was not a sad, childish desire to avoid the reality of heading out into the world but a genuine, heartfelt appreciation for what this sublime texture of work and expectation had done for me, and I did not want to leave my heavenly playground.

For only a fleeting but immortal second our eyes met and it was as though I knew what Father Hazelton had been trying to say to me all along. It seemed to permeate my whole body, down to the marrow of my bones, still not knowing how to put it in words at that time but feeling it alive and well inside of me. Chill bumps raced down my arms as he continued.

"Let us pray. Heavenly Father, today we give thanks for each of these boys, their lives and their contributions, big and small, to the community of St. Andrew's School. We ask that each one be blessed and rewarded with your grace and that we become aware of what their lives have meant to us, the teachers of St. Andrew's School. Father, as we prepare for parting this weekend, we ask to be guided today in the footsteps of your Son, Jesus Christ, so that our lives may be a blessing to this world and to You, to whom we owe praise and thanksgiving. We truly give thanks for these young men and what they have meant to us. It has been our privilege and honor serving them. But now, we must turn them over to you and your direction. Heavenly Father, they are our boys, too. Take good care of them. In Christ's name, we pray, Amen."

I was not emotional considering the fact that I was being kicked out of the cocoon. I felt marvelous and proud and wore my blazer with prowess and command.

As I was leaving with my family, Father Hazelton caught up with me, tucked an envelope in my pocket and said, "Don't read this until you leave campus. Promise?"

"Yes, sir. I promise." I fumbled around in my right pocket to make sure the note was safe and secured. It was burning a hole.

We hugged one another and I said, "I don't know what to say. There's so much I want to say. I can't thank you enough."

"You don't have to." he said, "Be safe, Billy, and live boldly and courageously. I wish you the best of luck. You will figure out how to speak to your mother when the time is right."

"I know I will. I'll miss you, Father. Thank you so much."

"Take care," he said as he drew away, disappearing around the corner.

The chapel was still emptying like cold syrup and it took a half hour before the parents had a chance to thank all of the teachers and speak with the priests who conducted the service. We stood defiantly on the asphalt pad in front of the chapel, not having a clue as to what to say to one another.

This last awkward goodbye brought on a flurry of confusing and strange remarks. We acted as if our verbal salads were sensible and attempted to maintain poise in the midst of this grand departure. But our condition showed through. Muttering meaningless and meandering nonsense, we stalled, hoping to escape time.

Cameras were clicking everywhere, thousands of pictures being snapped of every possible combination of faces and hand signs. It was a spectacular moment but it was goodbye.

Sammy and I had shipped our trunks a week before and the car had been packed that morning. I trotted back to my room one more time to see if anything had been left behind. It was physically bare. I paused and leaned against the two-man study desk, and faced the dressing mirror where my eyes centered in my own. I was forty pounds heavier than when I arrived.

I took a deep breath and surveyed the room that spoke with familiar morning sounds and smells of seasonal clothing, and let my left hand glide across the smooth laminated counter top. At that moment—and it wasn't until then—I was ready to leave and get on with it.

"It's hard to believe, isn't it?"

I swung around, taken off guard.

"Hey, Duck, I didn't hear you come in. Yeah, it is . . . seems like just yesterday."

"C'mon, we'll walk to the quad. My mom and dad are waiting on me."

Arm around each other, we left Hughston Hall for the last time. At the quad, we embraced.

"You ready to go?" he asked.

"Yes, I am," I said. "What about you?"

"Mac, I been here for five years. It's about all I know. But I'm ready for the new world. I'm ready to go out there and make another home somewhere."

"And make it, you will. I know you, Duck. You're tough. You're like my brother and I'll miss you. I don't know if we'll ever see one another again. I never go to Florida."

"Well, I don't ever come to North Carolina. But no sweat. We'll see one another again. We will. Take care of yourself, Billy McNeal," Duck said.

"Thanks for being my friend, Steven Larue."

"Thanks for being mine, Bill McNeal."

We hugged and Duck disappeared to catch up with his mom and dad.

Mother pulled the car around where Sam and I piled in. The car moved slowly away, enabling Sammy and me to see all of the faces one more time. The windows were rolled down, our upper torsos hanging out balancing on one hand, while the other slapped palms of passing classmates, waving, touching, for the last time.

Mother weaved her way past Father Henry's house and I took one last look at our mountain haven, one last earnest glance, spinning one last enduring tapestry to hold a lifetime of memories. My heart was afire.

The station wagon rolled out of the entrance heading for the interstate as I twisted to my side to get my jacket off. I felt something thick in the right pocket, removed it, and realized it was the envelope from Father Hazelton.

His hand-written message on personalized stationary was the last communication I would receive from him.

Billy,

Believe in yourself. What you believe influences the earth itself. But above all, know that you can rely on yourself—

your true, immortal Self. You must choose to learn of its power—carrying you into your own place, endowing you with your own true birthright. It protects and guards you, and shows you how to help others who need help. Constantly, remind yourself of this power by believing in yourself, knowing that the freedom you seek has come— freedom from mind and body.

Remember that love is not affection, neediness, or being friendly. Love is fearless, strong, and free. Love is the source of all things. It is the glue of life—all-encompassing, leaving no thing and no one out. Love is the light in the dark when all else has and will disappear before your very eyes. Love is the Holy Spirit. It is the Light in you. Billy, this is the path. This is the way to engage the obstacles of life. This is the way to heal the earth.

Billy, know that nothing can hurt you but your own perceptions. Your perceptions of others reveal to you who you consider yourself to be. See their unfolding as you learn to see your own. Have faith—unshakable certainty—that you will navigate the troubled waters of life for you do not walk alone. Learn to be still and listen to the voice inside, to your inner Self, not the self-limited world has taught you. This voice is a hand on your shoulder, an understanding you can trust that above all else that is taking away all your fear.

Billy, this is the time for your absolute trust of the future ahead even though you have no evidence that it will work out. Your conviction of His Presence is all-important. No fear, no loss, no doubt can come upon you when you are certain of His all-encircling Love. When everything in form disappears, love remains because it is eternal.

May the long-time sun shine upon you, Billy McNeal,

May God's love always surround you,
And may the clear voice within you,
Guide your way Home.

Love,
Father Hazelton

By the time I finished reading the contents of his letter several times, the sound of the tires quieted suddenly and I realized we were on I-24 heading back to North Carolina. For the duration of the trip, I did not speak to Sam or my mother. I rested with a heart satiated with the alluring magic of these men and the mountain I was leaving behind. I folded his letter, placed it in my wallet and closed my eyes.

PROLOGUE

The Regrets of an Absentee Father

As I turn fifty-two this year, I live a life of grace in the mountains of Western North Carolina where I work, helping others in the best way I know how.

I have lived through the reconciliation of my past and the mistakes I have made. I have experienced the love my father and stepfather had for me, however limited it was. It is not without the pain in mind that I am willing to acknowledge those circumstances for from them I was taught compassion and courage. And I have learned that this was my choice to make. There simply came a time that having forgiven myself and having released the shame, it was easy to forgive them. One precludes the need for the other.

I didn't meet my real father for the first time until I was thirty-eight years old. He was in a Charlotte hospital when a friend of his contacted me to ask if I would consider seeing him.

"Of course I will," I said.

"Bill, I need to tell you he is not expected to live. He is on his third bypass surgery and things are not looking very good. I can't tell you how much it will mean to him. You boys meant so much to him."

"It's my pleasure," I said. "I'll head over there tonight."

As I quietly entered his hospital room, he lay sleeping on his side, unveiling a worn and anguished face, a blueprint of strife.

I watched the absentee patriarch wrestle for his next thin breath, his chest contracting with the pain that each conditional reprieve brought. An alcoholic for thirty-eight years, one leg amputated, his path was ending.

After an hour of silent discovery and wishful thinking, he opened his eyes, studied me, and said, "Billy, you came."

"Yes, but how did you know it was me?" I asked smiling.

"I am your father. I know who you are," he said beaming.

There was a moment of indecision and then I spoke. "Are you OK?"

"No, I'm not," he said. "I'm afraid this is the end for me. I'm in so much pain."

"If this is the end, where would you like to start?" I asked clumsily.

"Let's start from the beginning. I want to hear about your life. I have heard that both of you did very well. I want to hear about it all."

"I'll tell you whatever you'd like to know but before I do, thanks for inviting me. It's really great having the chance to finally meet you."

"I decided that I would rather die in North Carolina. I want to be buried in the family grave." He paused for a moment.

"I had Jim call Sam but Sam won't have anything to do with seeing me. Sammy hates me," he said bluntly.

"It's important to allow him to be where he is. It's hard for him to hear. He has his own path through all of this," I said.

"You know, your mother had a right to pack my bags," he said, heaping the fiery ashes of a regretful past upon himself.

He was wasting no time getting to the core.

"I understand," I said.

He paused for a moment and allowed himself a breath of fresh air from the self-imposed prison in which he lived.

"I understand that Nolan was a good father to you boys, that he took care of you," he said. "I knew that you didn't really like him but I was so sorry to hear he died when both of you were still young."

"He did the best he could under the circumstances," I said, feeling no need to go into a past that that carried no more weight.

Thus, our five-hour evening journey began, not to survive into the tomorrow. As he began to cry at one point, he held my hand

and said, "I know you can never forgive me for having left you and your brother."

I smiled, squeezed his hand, and replied, "If you've come all the way from California to ask for my forgiveness, you wasted a trip. I forgave you a long time ago. To speak truthfully, I don't think that's the issue. The issue is that you can't forgive yourself and I don't think you're going to. Forgiving yourself precludes your needing mine. I promise you, I hold no ill feelings toward you. In fact, to be truly honest, there never was anything to forgive you for. It was just part of the dance this time around. We both missed a great chance at being together. And yes, it is true. You had two fine sons. But I promise that it's all OK."

"I have missed so much, so very much. I have gone through life without ever valuing what was important to me, without ever coming to terms with my drinking and the pain I caused."

I remained silent as he tried to gain his composure. He changed subjects and began speaking.

"How was school for you?" he asked. "I knew you and Sammy went off to St. Andrew's School. I kept up with you as best I could from the news that Tootie and Evelyn sent me. I heard you and Sam were quite the baseball players. You know, your great-grandfather Bull McNeal played baseball at Carolina. Baseball was in your blood."

"Baseball was great. I played at State for a while. It's funny. At the time I was at St. Andrew's, there were many times I was unhappy. I even tried to run away one time. But when I look back, it was probably the greatest thing that ever happened to me. I think I still continue to consolidate my learning during my two years there. I learned so much about myself. And baseball was great."

"I wish I had been able to be a part of that. I'm sure your mother made the right decision to send you there and look at you, just look at you. Your mother may have made mistakes but she got you educated . . . that's for sure. I'm so proud of you, of what you've become," he said, his face wrinkling under the weight and pressure of time and shame.

"Oh, I've made some damn stupid mistakes. I think I'm a slow learner but I'm getting there."

"Aren't we all?" he said. "Do you ever hear from any of your classmates or teachers from St. Andrew's?"

"No, not often. Every once in a while I catch news about some of them. Mr. Gautier, my French teacher, was actually responsible for getting me hired at St. Andrew's. I taught and coached there for several years but came back to North Carolina. Two of my friends from there have died since we graduated. A guy named Make and a kid named Harry. I don't really remember their real names. Everyone had nicknames. They were good guys."

"I was on the school's mailing list for the newsletter so I kept up as best I could. It didn't appear to be easy. Were the classes hard?"

"Not really, not if you studied. I realized as the years went by that I lived better and performed better in a disciplined space . . . better than just roaming around. There were a lot of habits I learned there that I practice to this day. I learned a lot about myself."

"Son, I've done a lot of roaming around in my life. A lot. In fact, there was a time I thought about becoming an Episcopal priest myself."

"I had several priests for teachers and a few monks, too. The priests were referred to as 'Fathers.' They were men who were ordained in the Episcopal Church. I think, all in all, it would be fair to say that they saved my life. I owe so much to them for what they did for me. I know that I will never, ever be able to repay them for what they did. I wouldn't even know how to start," I said. "In fact, I still carry in my wallet a letter that one of the fathers wrote to me when I graduated."

I reached for my wallet and pulled from it the worn letter from Father Hazelton, handing it to my father. As he read it, he began to cry.

"Counting me and the fact that you didn't get along with Nolan, I'd say, there had been an absence of men in your life up to that point. So, I say," he said with gratitude, "God bless the fathers of St. A., the men who took care of my boys when I could not. "

"Yes," I said, beginning to cry, "God bless the fathers of St. A."

"Billy, I'm so sorry I left you and your brother. I'm so sorry," he said, sobbing, collapsing again into the pain of this unbearable intersection in life.

"It's okay . . . I promise . . . it's okay," I said, my tears blurring my vision, choking my words.

"Son, you'll figure some way how, I know you will. Do it for me. You'll figure out some way to thank the men who took care of you. If you haven't already, I know you will."

"Yes, sir," I said. "I will."

We embraced, unwilling to relinquish the moment knowing that it would not last, that it would not survive the silence of this long, painful week.

My father died early the next morning but not before both of us courageously spoke of our paths, our truths, and forgiveness that both of us were seeking. Having been apart for thirty-eight years, he was still my father and I was still his son.

I called Mother the next day.

"Well, I guess you heard. He died," I said.

"Yes, I did hear," she replied.

There was silence.

"Well, I understand his funeral is Thursday. Would you like to go? You can go with me if you want. I already talked to Sam. He's not coming."

"Yes, I'd love to go," she explained. "As a matter of fact, I'll wheel his casket down Main Street if you want, just as long as he pays me back the money he owes me."

"You know, Mother, he did mention something about that," I said laughing.

I paused and said, "Let me see if I've got this right. It's been thirty-five years and you're still angry. Better still, enraged."

"Son, if you want to go, then go. But you'll go alone."

"Well," I said, "I thought it was appropriate to ask. I am still his son. So, I am going to his funeral. And alone I'll go."

A few friends from his past attended the brief ceremony. He was buried in his hometown of Monroe beside his sister, his mother and father, and grandparents who died before I was born. I drove home, thinking of Sam and the resentment he had learned well.

Sixteen years later, my four children from two marriages are blessings in my life who remind me daily of the father I, too, want to be. I wonder if I will ever be all that they want or need. It is next to impossible to share with them the precious life I have led and the blessings their mere presence has brought me. In the end, I hope it will have been enough for them.

Last week, Jonathan came to my office for his second visit, having been expelled from school for the remainder of the semester.

"It's too hard for me," he said. "I can't do this."

"No, it's not," I replied. "It isn't a question of your ability. It's a question of your willingness."

"You don't know me—you don't know what I've been through. If you knew, you'd know why I am the way I am," he said drifting into his shame.

"I want you to consider the possibility that I do know you and that I know that you are capable of great things once you get straightened out in your head who you are and who you're not."

"What do you mean?" he asked.

"I read the court report. I know the background you come from and I know that you're much bigger than that. I know you're capable of dealing with this and becoming what you can be. You are so smart, so talented."

"How do you know?" he asked.

"Because no one can be an idiot and make an A in Algebra II," I said, holding up the report.

"My old man tells me I'm going to end up in jail."

"Your old man's right," I said. "If the circumstances don't change, if you're not willing, you will end up in jail."

"I've already been arrested twice. I don't want to end up in prison," he said, beginning to cry.

"Good! That's a great start! And now that we know where you don't want to end up, where do you want to end up?" I asked.

"I don't know," he said.

"That's OK. We can talk about that. But I want you to know

something, Jonathan. This whole thing, this dance of life, this bullshit we go through in growing up . . . it's OK. It's worth the struggle. But, Jonathan, listen to me. You don't have to keep pulling these lame stunts. You can create anything you want. But nothing is going to change until you do. Nothing is going to change until you choose for it to change. If you want to be at the top, you've got to act like you're on the top."

"I need to get back in school. I don't want to end up working at McDonald's for the rest of my life."

"Then, let's get back in school right away and be ready to go at semester. Let's get focused and figure out what we're going to do."

Two hours later, Jonathan left, our embrace leaving both of us connected and more certain of tomorrow.

As I began to close the door, he stepped back in. "Dr. McNeal, thanks for helping me out."

"Think nothing of it," I said. "It's the reason I'm here."

"I'll see you next week," Jonathan said.

"Next week," I said, waving goodbye.

Tonight, I am home and go to bed a blessed man, sinking into the bliss of my limitless and exploding joy. As I recount my life, it is more joy than I can contain and more pain than is possibly bearable. It is a peace that embraces the tragic and the divine, holding the paradox of living and dying, of sleeping and waking, with delicate assurance of yet another day, another chance to change my mind about who I am and what I am doing here. It is claiming the power to bring good out of evil, hope from hopelessness, meaning from absurdity, and finding again what was at one time lost. This is my dance.

Tonight, my loving wife lies in my arms, and stroking my face, she whispers, "You are my phoenix and I am so proud of you."

"Sarah, I love you so much. And at last, I am proud of me, too."

I smile and lose myself in her eyes and the love that embraces our home.

"Did you see Jonathan again today?" she asks.

"Yes . . . for about two hours."

"Is he going to be OK?" she asks. "He's seems to be a very talented young man."

"Yes, he is talented and he's going to be fine. A little time, a little pressure, a little pain. He's got what it takes. They're all good kids. They just don't know it."

We give thanks for our life together and begin to breath our way into another night of peace and gratitude of just being alive, of another precious day with one another.

At last, I am invulnerable, my heart yearning to live forever, as I worship the mystery of becoming and the fire of awakening. At last, I am certain.

As I close my eyes, I roar my deep and ever-lasting gratitude to the fathers of St. A. as I quietly hum.

> We're the boys of old St. A.
> And we don't give a damn.
> We go to school and break the rules
> And flunk the damn exams.
> So, to hell with the East,
> To hell with the West,
> To hell with the whole damn crew,
> If you don't go to old St. A., to hell, to hell with you.